SCARRED

THE RUTHLESS REBELS MC SERIES BOOK 3
CHELSEA CAMARON
RYAN MICHELE

1st edition published: May 19, 2017

Cover Design by: M.L. Pahl of IndieVention Designs

Editing by: Asli Fratarcangeli

Proofreading: Silla Webb

This work of fiction is intended for mature audiences only. All sexually active characters portrayed in this book are eighteen years of age or older. Please do not buy if strong sexual situations, violence, domestic abuse, and explicit language offends you.

This is not meant to be an exact depiction of life in a motorcycle club, but rather a work of fiction meant to entertain.

Kimberly Roe, our girl! You have been with us for years. You make us smile and keep us encouraged. Thank you for your awesomeness. To time outs, overwhelming schedules, and random late night texts.

JOIN US

Come join Chelsea Camaron and Ryan Michele in our groups on Facebook
Chelsea Camaron
Ryan Michele

Want to be up to date on all New Releases? Sign up for our Newsletter
Chelsea Camaron
Ryan Michele

SCARRED (RUTHLESS REBELS MC #3)

Whitton 'Skinny' Thorne – scarred skin only covers a beautiful soul.

Bitter with a capital B.

Life has been hell from the beginning when Whitton was burned as an infant, yet as much as he pushes me away I'm always coming back for more.

When I finally let go, he wants to let me in. How do I survive when we've both been scarred?

Chelsea Camaron and Ryan Michele have teamed up to bring you an explosive new MC romance that will have you panting for more of the Ruthless Rebels. Hold on tight, it's going to be a wild ride full of action and suspense that these two authors are known for. Throw in two people who finally get their second chance, and things are about to get smoking hot.

CHAPTER 1

FAIRYTALES, NURSERY RHYMES, AND CHILDHOOD MEMORIES—NONE OF THEM ARE REALLY ALL THAT GREAT!

Roe

*H*olding my hand in the air with three fingers up, I sing the song about Sally the camel and her humps. Simple.

I don't have or need complications in my life. Sally has humps that come and go, she has issues; me—I'm good.

The nineteen smiling children sing along with me with utter enthusiasm. They love this song. Most days we sing it once, sometimes twice, before we do the weather and calendar first thing in the morning. Our routine, the structure the kids need to thrive, and I need to feel like things are in order.

I look up when the door to my classroom opens.

It's preschool. The director of the school comes in and out throughout the day so, at first, I don't think much of it. When my assistant teacher, Ms. Jennifer, stands up to take over, it's then I make my way to the door. As the lead teacher, if the director comes in, Jennifer takes over for me and I meet with my boss. Any changes necessary from the director, I will make them. Jennifer and I have worked together for three years now, our system is solid.

Beside the director, Ms. Marie, is the cutest little girl. Obviously, this visit is to bring us a new student. Her blue eyes are a bit too big for her face making those rounded little cheeks stand out too. There isn't fear in her blue depths, but there is a lot going on in that brain of hers. Finishing the song to the delight of the children on the ABC carpet, I let Jennifer continue with the next song. I focus my attention and greet our newest student, warm smile in place.

I bend down to her level, looking her in the eyes. "Hello, I'm Ms. Roe, and what's your name?"

"Marlayna," the little girl in pigtails says softly.

My heart breaks when I see the scar on her neck that her hair isn't covering. I know those marks too well. I fight back the emotion that sits just under the surface.

Burns.

This little girl has suffered a tragedy, and I hate that for her.

"Would you like to join us in circle time?" I offer as I fight back the past. *He* is not the only person to be burned in their lives and survive. So many things twist inside me, and I have to push it down. The emotions that keep beating down the well-structured walls I've built around them over the years always try to spill over, but I won't allow it. I've had no other choice but to keep a handle on it all.

My job is about teaching and nurturing Marlayna. Today is not about him or his scars.

She nods her head and the day commences with story time, rhyme time, nap time, and all the normal activities of my day. Marlayna adjusted very well in the class for it being her first day. She went with the flow with no trepidation and without much of a reaction to anything.

It pains me. I don't like when the kids cry, but when they come in almost numb like little Marlayna it hurts more to wonder what has hardened them to life already. Children should be free to be kids, not caught up in some adult situation or punished unnecessarily.

The afternoon passes with little Marlayna quickly falling into the routine and making friends. After each of the children are gone and I get my room cleaned up, I head out.

Arriving home, I sit in the sunroom of my two-bedroom house and enjoy the Georgia afternoon. When I moved out, this was my one requirement—sunroom. I love the outdoors and not feeling closed up.

Blakely, Georgia, population five thousand. Small town lifestyle near the Alabama – Georgia state lines.

April is my favorite month of the year. The weather is sunshine, the birds sing, and the humidity isn't unbearable so boob sweat is a non-issue for the time being. No woman ever wants boob sweat. August, in the deep south is hotter than hell, so I'll enjoy my outside time while I can.

In fact, tomorrow I think I'll take my class to have a picnic and maybe do sidewalk chalk and hopscotch on the playground. They love the outside, and it helps to get as much of their energy out as possible.

My mind goes to little Marlayna. Her file tells a story that breaks my heart. She is in the system. Foster care, with the Brown family, who are regulars in the community when it comes to taking in children. They will be good to her.

I once knew a boy who lived with the Browns'. My mind, my heart, they always go back to him. I wish it wouldn't but we have too much shared between us. His scars were similar to hers only they covered part of his face and half his body.

Whitton Thorne, the boy down the road with a tortured past. His mom had things so twisted in her head when it came to her twin boys. She believed Whitton was evil and Waylon was the son of Jesus or something crazy. I wasn't privy to all the details. I just know every time the state let the boys go back to her, Whitton was returned to his social worker more damaged than before. I know once they tried to send Waylon back and leave Whitton with the Browns' only for Waylon to run away to be with his twin. The two of them were close. In their situation, I would imagine one would have to be. They were also complete opposites. In school Whitton was quiet, while Waylon was confident and spoke to everyone. As we grew up, Whitton kept his calm, always focused on school. Waylon, he got more aggressive, which sometimes got him into trouble. Waylon drew everyone's attention, it's like he commanded it. He was always in control. Whitton, he didn't care who knew him, paid attention to him, or gave a single second glance in his direction. He drew me in, though. There wasn't a move he made that didn't captivate me.

God, I loved Whitton.

From the beginning, when he was the boy I bumped into in grade school to the man who he grew into, there isn't a moment in time since I met Whitton Thorne that he didn't have my attention. He intrigued me. His strength captivated me. And the more time I had with Whitton Thorne in my life, the harder I fell in love with him.

Even now, years have passed, and I can't help but hope he's okay. Hope that, somewhere, he found his slice of happy.

Night comes and I slide into my t-shirt blend sheets. I don't make much with my job, but this is my splurge, soft bed sheets. After all, one can't be at their best with twenty children without a good night sleep. I close my eyes, and the fatigue of the day quickly consumes me.

"Whitton Thorne, one day you're gonna be the President." I smile proudly at my friend.

"The President of the rejects club, maybe," he replies in his normal tone.

I sigh. The boy is nothing short of amazing. He's smart, athletic, and cute. He just doesn't see it. Him and his twin brother look nothing alike. All the girls crush on Waylon. He has this mystery to him. Whitton, though; Whitton is the kind of boy you can talk to, really talk to. There is depth to him. The intrigue of him keeps me on edge to know more, see more, and have more time with him. From the time we met in elementary school, at eight-years-old, until now, he has captured my attention. We're young, he's seventeen and I'm sixteen, but I can't get enough of him.

"What do you see in me, Roelyn Duprey?"

I feel the blush cover my cheeks. "All good, I see all the good in you, Whitton."

He smirks. "You got the wrong Thorne, Roe. Maybe you think I'm Waylon."

I prop my hand on my hip. "I know what I see in you, Whitton, and I see potential!"

"You have all the potential, Roe. The future is in front of you, and there's not a single thing to hold you back," he tells me like he does all the time. "You need to have bigger and better than what Blakely, Georgia and a misfit like me can offer."

"Oh, Whitton, you will have bigger and better in your life. I know it."

He laughs me off like he does every single time I tell him I think he'll be someone someday. Only thing is, I know down to my soul he has so much more to give in this world. My heart bleeds that he doesn't see it.

My alarms blares drawing me out of the dream. The memory of a lost time when things weren't complicated and the boy I knew and believed in may not have believed in himself, but back then he believed in me. Something I desperately needed.

Whitton Joseph Thorne, my best friend since we ran into each other playing at recess when we were only eight-years-old. Twenty years later, I still consider him the best friend I've ever had … only everything between us has changed.

No longer is he the boy I thought could give the world goodness. He's a grown man who left everything in Georgia behind ten years ago when we crossed a line.

Would I cross the line again? If I knew the outcome would be this, I'm not so sure. At the time, it felt right. Hell, I thought it was going to change everything into something we could build a future on.

Except, Waylon took off and Whitton was right behind him. Where one brother went, the other was sure to follow. They had a rough start in life. Bonded as twins, bonded as brothers, and bonded by the times life kicked them while they were down. Those two would always stick together.

Part of me blames Waylon. The other part of me knows the truth. Whitton ran. Yes, he woke up after the best night of our lives and couldn't handle the emotion. He found out Waylon took off, and he followed. It was an escape and an all too easy excuse.

I'm not sure he realized that no matter the distance he put between us, he still had me with him. I haven't figured out a way to get that piece of me back from Whitton yet. Even after all these years, I belong to him in a way that keeps me from moving on.

Looking at little Marlayna yesterday and waking up today, it's time I let go of Whitton. Everything I thought we could one day be is a far-fetched dream. Marlayna has her life ahead of her. No matter the past, she has a future.

13

The same can be said for Whitton Thorne, and it's a future that he decided would be without me.

~

SITTING DOWN TO A LATE DINNER, I pull out my phone and scroll social media. I don't know why because it only tells me things I don't care to know. Even with a bowl of vegetable soup in front of me, my stomach growls at seeing the yummy chocolate desserts. I have a sweet tooth. My ass and hips thank me for it.

Sipping my soup, it warms me. My thumb moves on my phone screen, skipping past people I went to high school with that I never talk to. Why I'm even friends with them, I'll never know. Maybe it's time to declutter my life. Most of the time, people friend you just to see what you're doing and then delete you. Personally, I like it when people take out their own trash.

My private message pops up, and internally I groan seeing it's from Lance. *Hi. See you're on. Want to talk to you.* He types. I need to figure out how to block people from seeing when I'm on and when I'm not. Or maybe I just need to block him. I'm thinking the latter.

Going out with Lance was up there with many mistakes I made in my life. Two dates, then I called it off. Only he didn't seem to get the point. Even telling him flat out—I wasn't interested—he still messages me, texts me, and calls me. Not wanting to appear rude, I've answered all of them. But this, I just don't want to engage with him. I'm tired of it. I repeat myself all day, everyday, with my students. My personal life, I don't want that.

I move the little bubble that shows a picture of a golf club, Lance, and toss it down below to get rid of it off my screen.

The phone begins to ring, and I jump. First thought is, Lance is calling me. Then when I look at the screen, I see *Elizabeth Calling*. A smile crosses my face as I accept the call.

"Hey, woman!" I greet my best friend. We met in college, which seems like a lifetime ago, but really wasn't.

"Hey, back at ya! What are you doing? I want to meet for drinks."

I look at the clock noting it's only five-thirty, but I do have to work tomorrow. Drinking and then rowdy children in the morning is not a good combination.

"Is something up?" I take the last bite of my soup and push it to the side.

"Yes, but I don't want to tell you over the phone. Meet me in twenty at Carlyle's?"

Looking down at my clothes, the puppy dog pajama bottoms won't cut it going out. "Give me thirty. I need to change."

"Epp," She makes the sound then says, "Okay, see you then," and disconnects. Whatever she has in store must be exciting.

At least one of us has something good going on.

CHAPTER 2

FLAMES EXTINGUISH, SCARS FADE, BUT THE BURN CAN'T BE FELT FOREVER!

Skinny

I strike the match and watch it burn.

The blends of reds and yellows into oranges is mesmerizing. The flickers of colors all move as if they're dancing together. The heat gets closer and closer to my fingertips as the flame grows intently.

I feel no pain. I feel nothing.

Void. Empty.

My life is not one of colors and blends.

Poof. I blow the match out. The flame is extinguished. All that's left is black smoke. It's like my soul. Dark, unforgiving.

I sit in the dim lit room I call home. Ruthless Rebels MC–my family and the clubhouse where I calm myself at the end of every day.

The ten by ten foot space has my bed, one nightstand, and a dresser. The closet is small, but I keep a three-tiered bookshelf in there, full of different books and photo albums. It's not much, but it's mine. Beside that door is the door to the bathroom.

Feeling the acid burn in my gut, I get up and make my way in front of the porcelain. Dropping to my knees I wretch.

I don't remember the last time I woke up and didn't throw up within an hour. It happens every damn day. I finish, stand, wash up and brush my teeth. There's no use in looking in the mirror, I already know the mess I'll see.

I hate fucking mirrors. Only one time in my life did I ever look in a mirror and not see the hideous beast I am ... and that will never happen again. Roelyn Duprey, she made the man in the mirror. Not a monster, but a lover. She is everything beautiful I should never touch. It's a memory I'll hold onto.

She believed in me, believed in having something not understanding the monster I am. From the beginning, the devil gripped my heart and never let go. The bitch known as my mother told me I was spawned in evil. She scarred me, marked me, and made sure the world could see me for what I am. A horrible, vile, demonized man.

Roelyn Duprey had rose colored glasses on. I let her keep them on because I needed her lifeline. The spark between us, I fed. Continuing to fuel, provide the heat, like a flame. I watched us grow, flicker, and rather than watch us fade, at the peak of the fire burning between us, I snuffed it out quickly leaving nothing behind but black smoke.

My brother needed me and Roe needed me to go away, even if she didn't know it. I took off, never looked back, and haven't looked in a mirror since the night I watched myself fuck her in one.

Spitting in the sink, I rinse my mouth, and walk away never checking my reflection. I know what I'd see. The flames of hell flicker in my eyes and burn in my soul, no need to remind myself.

Throwing on a clean pair of jeans, I don't bother with boxers, briefs, or anything to cover my junk. The raw denim rub will remind me I'm alive. Somehow, in the hell that is my life, I keep surviving and I'm not sure why. Sliding on my shirt, I grab my cut as I drop my feet into my boots before I head out, not bothering to tie the laces till I get to my bike.

Today I have packing duty. I don't mind. I'll head to the warehouse, pack the guns to ready for shipment, and then meet up with Waylon.

My twin, Waylon, or Triple Threat—TT, as he's known in the club—is everything I'm not. He's good looking, level-headed, and not held back by a damn thing.

Me—I'm a scarred mess, hot-head, and haunted by the one thing I gave up so long ago.

Yeah, tonight calls for the strip club. I'll pay to have a stranger grind on me till I get hard, then head back to the clubhouse and fuck a trick until I can't remember my name, my past, and the woman I left behind.

∽

"IT'S A BOY!" Shamus rushes into the clubhouse announcing. "DJ has a healthy, happy, eight pound, nine ounce, twenty-two inch baby boy. Kenderly is doing good."

There are smiles and happiness that fill the space. Shamus comes over to me, slapping me on the back. "You wanna go with us to set up the house, brother."

I nod. There isn't a single thing with any of my brothers I would miss because they're all I have. And for once in my life, I belong.

After DJ's whore mother dropped her problems on Kenderly's doorstep, DJ claimed his woman and, in turn, the Rebels handled their shit. Kenderly and her mother had an uphill battle to climb with everything they had already lost, but DJ's mother cost them their home.

It took some time, but DJ won over Kenderly's heart. They have a good life, building themselves a solid future. And now their new addition. Everything is looking good for my Rebels' brother.

Not too long ago, DJ bought them a big ass house and furnished it to Kenderly's liking. Now, it's time for the Rebels to ride in and make sure our newest member is set.

"Your woman handle buying the goods?" I ask Shamus, knowing he and Andrea have decided not to have kids because of the health risks for her.

"Shit, brother. She loves shopping for all this baby crap. Kitten has a soft spot for being the auntie, apparently. She even bought Kenderly a video baby monitor instead of the basic one they had on the registry."

I laugh. "Nothing wrong with that."

"I didn't think so but, apparently, DJ and Kenderly had talked. DJ didn't want to be fuckin' his woman and look to the nightstand and see their baby awake."

"I never thought a damn thing would give DJ stage fright." We both laugh before heading out to go set up a nursery Rebels style.

"Guess a baby changes things. I'm good with how my life is; no change needed here," Shamus adds with a smirk. Things are good in the club, they are good for DJ and Shamus. It's even better to feel like I'm a part of something real.

Andrea is already inside when Shamus, Lurch, Triple Threat, and I pull up. She rushes outside and over to the car parked in front of the house.

"Mom brought me over, got lots to unload," she says more to Shamus than anyone with a smile that is relaxed and easy going.

Given the path Andrea went through to finally be okay again and with Shamus, I smile with her. Like me, her life is full of scars.

Only, in all the turmoil, Andrea has found a way to not allow her scars to define her.

She lived a different life. Following her dreams into investigative reporting landed her half dead in a hospital oceans away from her home. She survived her traumatic brain injury like I survived my burns. With no place to go to pick up the pieces, she came home. It took a bit, but Shamus and Andrea worked their shit out. Their past isn't holding them back from a future.

TT and I won't have this. Our past defines our future, and it's not one that looks so bright.

For a moment, I had hope that somehow I could have a second chance to have something real in my life outside of the club. With DJ and Shamus both getting their second chances, I thought maybe there would be a sliver of time where TT and I could have more than what we have managed to secure. Then I dreamt I caught a look in the mirror and quickly remembered what my life has been destined to be from the moment I was born.

I am my brother's keeper. My place on Earth is to protect him even from himself. I don't have the time or emotion for anything else.

Our mother is a psycho bitch who thinks my brother is the second coming of her God or some shit. Apparently, during an ultrasound, it appeared that I, baby b, was kicking or hitting baby a—being Waylon. From that moment on I was destined to the damned.

She even tried to have me aborted, but the doctors said she was too far along and it was risk to my brother. Then we were born.

She tried to leave me at the hospital. The nurses told her it wasn't good for infant twins to be separated this early. According to the medical records we later dug up, they felt she was suffering from postpartum depression and the doctor felt she would eventually want me. Having two babies at once, via c-section, meant she couldn't hold us right away so she didn't bond properly, the doctor noted.

Bond.

What a joke. The woman tried to kill me more than once.

I've never had a mother's love. Neither has my brother.

She may have wanted me marked, condemned, banished, and branded, but she wanted my brother to be some savior to the world.

We just wanted to be boys. We grew into men who just wanted to live life. To this day, I still can't understand her mindset. I gave up a long time ago trying. TT–that's another story.

I'll go to the ends of the Earth for my brother. I'll protect him from her, or God himself, if I have to.

"Snap out of it, these diapers won't unload themselves!" TT says, throwing a box of the shit holders at me.

"How many boxes do they think Kenderly needs?" I ask looking at the van full.

"Daisy, Gloria, Andrea, her mom, Kenderly's mom and aunt, and every other woman around swear they will go through these and more," Shamus says, walking inside with a bag of clothes.

"Wonder what it was like for mom to have twins?" TT says out loud, and my chest stings in the pain I know he feels.

Yeah, we have no future like what DJ or Shamus have found. I need to stop disillusioning myself into ever thinking I could. Walk the line, it's what I have to do.

If I fuck up, I'm not the only one who suffers, TT will too. I won't do that to him or me. Yes, I'm better off alone.

CHAPTER 3

LOCKS ARE MADE FOR DOORS BUT SHOULD BE MADE FOR HEARTS!

Roe

The children stand at the large tables covered in newspaper. Most of them have either paint or glue on every inch of their exposed arms. Thank goodness for smocks. I love to have a free for all day where the kids can express themselves. Sometimes, they'll tell you more with their creations than words that come from their mouths.

"Marlayna, how are you doing?" I bend to her level, it always helps to get their undivided attention. She's been doing so well these past two weeks. Adjustment is hard for most children, but I've learned that Marlayna has moved a lot since she was two. She's lived with five different foster care families and had trial runs with her biological parents. Each time she went to her parents she's been taken away. I can't imagine how this impacts her on the inside. One thing I can say, the girl hides it on the outside.

"I made a house." She points to the glop of paint on her large paper. It's green with yellow swirls, glitter and a few foam shapes added in for flowers.

"I like the colors and the shapes you made."

She smiles, but it's small. The one thing I haven't seen much of is her smile, but I have hope.

"I'm gonna have a house like this." Her light brown hair is in a ponytail today and bobs as she talks. "And they're gonna be big locks on the doors, and no one can come in."

I avoid looking at the marks on her neck. I don't want to make her uncomfortable and most of all, my heart, my emotions have to stay in check for my job.

My heart clenches remembering that same wish when I was younger. *If only it had a lock.* All this sweet little girl wants out of life is a house with a lock. She wants to feel safe and protected. So much innocence and I just want to wrap her in a bubble and keep her away from everything and everyone.

"That's a great idea."

"Yep," she says proudly. "And I'm gonna dance like I do at Mrs. Brown's house. She just turns on the music, and I can dance wherever I want."

A smile graces my face thinking about this little girl dancing all around a house feeling safe, loved, and appreciated. All children should be given that in life. Unfortunately, so many don't.

"Sounds like you have a plan."

I remember when I was younger and used to plan my future. Nothing is how I ever thought it would be. Things may not have gone according to plan, but I have a job I absolutely love and feel like I make a difference. In the end, I may not have everything I wanted, but I have something. In a world where so many have nothing, I'll hold onto the little things I managed to find.

She shrugs and a sad look sprinkles her eyes. She turns, picks up the paintbrush, and begins her work again. I clearly know when I've been dismissed. That's okay because every day she gives me a little more of herself. That right there is a treasure I hold dear.

I rise and announce, "Five more minutes. You have five more minutes to wrap up what you have. Five minutes." Repeating myself over and over is a part of my life. Most of the time it'll take me saying those words ten or twenty times before the little ones will finally get to where we need to be. Every day is a challenge, but I love it and would have it no other way. After clean up and lunch, it's time to rest.

Nap time is supposed to be quiet time. It's supposed to be when I can get all my state required paperwork done on all my children. It's supposed to be a time when I can get my lesson plans and prep done for the next week. It's not. No, I spend after-hours time doing those things. There are so many things that go with my job besides the time with the kids. If seeing them grow and learn wasn't so rewarding for me, it wouldn't be worth it for everything we have to do. Watching a child master something new, overcome a fear, being a part of their childhood memories—it's all worth more than money can ever buy.

Today, it's raining, so no outside time; which means the kids still have energy. It takes a lot of patting backs, reminders to stay on cots, and a few prayers above to get them to sleep, which is where all my prep time flies. Although the clock tells me that I only have fifteen minutes before I have to wake the little ones up, I suck in those minutes getting a recharge for the afternoon.

The door to my room opens and Ms. Marie is there. She waves me to come to her, and I look to my assistant who nods telling me she's fine with the children.

Stepping over the cots is a bit of a challenge, but I make it and step outside the door. The slow click echoes through the hallway. A woman with dark brown hair that falls down her shoulders and wire rimmed glasses stands there. She's dressed in a professional skirt and button-up blouse.

"Ms. Roe, this is Mrs. Easton. She's Marlayna's case worker."

The woman extends her hand and smiles warmly. "Nice to meet you, but I'm sorry they are under these circumstances."

I go on instant alert as she releases my hand. Inside I'm jittery. Normally, any meetings with a child's case worker, social worker, special education services are planned way ahead of time.

Her face is somber. She hesitates, and my heart rate picks up. "The Browns' were in a car accident. Mr. Brown died on impact, and Mrs. Brown is in ICU. They are unable to take care of Marlayna; I need to take her with me."

"Take her where?" I jump a little too quickly.

"I'll take her to the group home in Keensaw, Georgia for the time being."

"She has to come to school." When she shakes her head, my stomach hollows. Keensaw, Georgia is on

28

the other side of the county and not in our district. She's making progress here … with me. I've had to let a lot of children go over the years as they grow up, move on, and some even having to be shuffled in a system that is overrun. This one, well, it hurts and it hurts deeper than ever before.

"She'll attend school close to the home if they have a program." Even if stomping my foot wouldn't help anything I want to do it. It's not mandatory that children go to preschool, it's optional. Therefore, Marlayna could be sitting in a room day in and day out or in daycare.

"Can she stay with me?" I gasp as the words leave my mouth realizing what I just said. Me, taking on a child? My mind scrambles for something, anything, but it whirls for a moment.

"The facility is a private run, church owned establishment. We have over fourteen thousand cases in the state of Georgia and only around four thousand foster parents trained and approved. Marlayna isn't established in a school district like our older teens; it's easier to move her than the other children the Browns' had in their care," Mrs. Easton explains, and my heart shatters for all of these children, but most especially Marlayna.

"There has to be something I can do for her." Each word pains me as it leaves my mouth. My heart is shattering into a thousand pieces.

"I'm sorry, Ms. Roe, but the foster parent program is a lengthy one that you will need to go through. Unfortunately, we don't have that time in this moment. I need to take her."

I beg as I fight back tears. "Please don't."

The thought of her being alone again, when she just found a safe place to live breaks my heart. I was her. I see me in her. There's so much potential for her in this life. I overcame because of the people who came into my life. She can too, but she needs good people and a solid home not continual change.

"I'm sorry, but this is a must. You can come and visit her if you'd like. And, if you really want to do the foster parent paperwork, we can discuss it."

There's not much about my job that I hate, but this … this is at the top of my list. I have no other choice. My hands are tied. I haven't felt this helpless in a long damn time.

"I'm a foster parent, can I keep her?" Ms. Marie says, and my eyes shoot to her in surprise. "My husband and I have only had one child come through our doors, but we are approved."

Looking expectantly at Mrs. Easton, hope blossoms.

"Ms. Marie would take excellent care of her. I can attest to it." My mouth rambles on so quickly there's no stopping it. "She's great with kids. Runs this center so well it's won awards."

Mrs. Easton holds up her hand. "I'll see what I can do, but right now I have to take Marlayna with me. It's state policy and I can't change that, but if you give me your information, Ms. Marie, I'll see what I can do."

My heart hammers in my chest knowing that I have to get that little girl and give her over to this woman. The twist in my chest is painful, and I hope

Ms. Marie can get her and quickly so she doesn't feel like she's lost another place in her life.

Quietly, I enter the room and move through the little blue cots, coming to the sleeping angel. Her hands are tucked under her cheek and a small Barbie blanket is wrapped around her lower half.

Sucking in a deep breath, I sit on the floor and begin to rub her back. "Marlayna, it's time to wake up," I soothe, fighting back my emotions.

It takes a bit, but her eyes finally open. She yawns and stretches her little arms, the sleeves of her shirt riding up.

"Hey, bright eyes, I need you to come with me."

She sits up immediately and looks around the room very alert. Her eyes catch on the woman standing next to Ms. Marie then back to me. "Where?"

"Come and we'll talk."

She looks at Mrs. Easton then back at me. "Something happened." Damn, for only being four-years-old she's so damn intelligent at reading situations. That's wonderful, yet sad for the reasons she's had to learn that particular skill.

"Yes, something has. Let's go…,"

"No!" she shouts. The room begins to stir just from that one loud word.

"Calm down. It'll work out." I don't want to lie to her and tell her everything is going to be okay, because I have no idea if it will be. Hell, I don't know what tomorrow or the next minute will bring. Her panic only makes my emotions go into overdrive more.

"I'm not going to Mrs. Brown's house, am I?" she asks, quieting her tone and realizing what's going on as she becomes more awake. The sad look on her face has me wanting to reach out to her and wrap her in my arms, but I don't. If she needs that from me, she'll let me know.

"No, Marlayna. Mr. and Mrs. Brown were in an accident. Mrs. Easton, over there, is going to take you to a big house with lots of other kids."

The little girl closes her eyes and lets out a breath. Damn, I swear she's a twenty-year-old trapped in a four-year-old body. I know what it is to have to grow up way too fast, and it breaks my heart that she's endured her circumstances so young in life.

She moves to get up and reaches for the blanket. "Can I take this?" she asks, all the while I'm breaking inside, shattering every piece of my heart on the tiled floor of my classroom. I've had pain in my life, lots of it. This right here, letting this little girl go and possibly never seeing her again, is the worst.

As a teacher, I should be used to kids coming and going. But this little one wormed her way deep and it kills.

"Of course." She slips on her little shoes and stands up. I do as well, dusting off my bum. Wordlessly, Marlayna goes over to her cubby and pulls the papers out. Then goes to her book bag and stuffs everything in it. She puts on her coat and then her book bag, never once asking for any help, even when she struggles and I step forward—she steps back.

She walks past me. "Bye, Ms. Roe." Her voice is quiet, but her head is up as she walks over to Mrs. Easton who gives her a big smile. Mrs. Easton leads her out of the room by holding her hand. Once they get to the door, Marlayna turns back once more and those eyes will haunt my dreams.

I give a small wave and try to smile the best I can. Marlayna turns and walks out the door. I dart from the room, enter the teachers' lounge bathroom, and lock the door. I sit on the toilet and let my emotions spill over and fall to the floor. Looking at the lock, I cry harder and hope wherever Marlayna ends up, she'll have a lock on her door.

CHAPTER 4

IN A BATTLE OF GOOD VERSUS EVIL, NO ONE REALLY WINS!

Skinny

"Church," TT calls, slapping a hand on my shoulder as I sit staring at a box ready for transport.

Immediately, I stand and follow my brother out to our bikes. Typically, church is scheduled weekly, but when something important happens Thumper will call church unexpectedly like this.

We file into the room off the back of the clubhouse. Each patched member taking his place, Thumper slams the gavel down.

"New order of business," he explains and looks to Lurch.

"We got a client, boys. A new one," Lurch begins looking at each of us. "We're not sure we want to do business with the man." He sits back in his chair rubbing his beard. "Not sure we want to turn away his money, either. Think we need to scope the area and the individual."

Thumper and Lurch look at TT and me. "Blakely, Georgia."

My gut churns. The acid inside me burns and bubbles threatening to spill over.

TT shakes his head.

"Know it's a lot to ask, but LaRoche is offering up some serious green backs to become his supplier."

"Why the suspicion?" I ask, wondering what intel has already come in to put Thumper and Lurch on edge.

"Owns a pawn shop. No need for guns that he can't sell," Thumper informs the room. "You two spent some time in Blakely. You'll know the best ways to see what's going down without actually being seen."

I nod, knowing that going back to Georgia is the last thing my brother or I want to do, but it's also our duty to the club to follow orders.

"I bought us a window of time. Finish up your shit for this week. Next week you scan the area, the business, and the schedule LaRoche keeps. We'll reconvene and make a decision after your update."

~

"BROWNS' DIED," TT says, coming up to me in the clubhouse the day after we find out we have to go back to Georgia. Could shit get any deeper? What's left of the charred mess of my heart shatters and breaks. Not many people gave a damn about me and my brother. Most cast us off as *hard to handle delinquents*, but not the Browns'. I sure as shit don't know what they saw in my brother and me, but it was something.

The way they pushed us to do better than we thought we could in school. Mrs. Brown would sit at the table and help me with my homework, something my real mother never did. Hell, I was lucky to get a meal from my mother.

Not at the Browns'. Food was on the table for breakfast, lunch, and dinner. There was no wondering where my next meal would come from, not with them. Not only that, Mrs. Brown made both my brother and me help her cook. Granted, we both thought she was nuts, but we went along with it. Sometimes we even had fun. Especially the time we had a food fight in her kitchen. Mrs. Brown was the one who started it. It was one of my prized times with the Browns' because I didn't have much to smile about, except for Roe.

"How?" I ask as my emotions threaten to swallow me whole.

"Car accident. Mr. died on impact, Mrs. held on for a while, but she's lost, too." Triple Threat's face is blank, like it always is. I'm not sure what it would take to get him to feel again. Not that it matters. Hell, nothing matters at this point, except the club.

"When's the funeral?"

His sharp eyes cut to mine. "I'll find out, but I'm not goin'."

"Didn't expect you to. We're already goin' next week. No need for you to go twice." I know better to ever think he'd go back there. Not because of the Browns', but it's too close to our mother. We keep tight tabs on her because knowing where that wicked woman is, is a must. She needs to be put down, but for some reason, we just can't do it. There'll come a time, though. That I can guarantee.

"No sense in you goin' back for it either. That place is just full of shit." He sits on the stool up against the bar and takes a pull on his beer. "Nothin' there."

He's right. There isn't anything in Georgia for us but anger, and for me, one regret. Except when I close my eyes tight, I can see Mrs. Brown's soft smile and Mr. Brown's kind eyes, and I know I owe them my respects.

"I'm goin'," I decree, moving away from him and heading outside, needing to finish packing the guns for a separate order that came in on the fly.

Truth be told, I just need to get the fuck away, alone. Too many thoughts. Too many emotions. I hate every single one of them. I need some time on the open road alone with my bike and my mind.

My brother and I didn't get a great start in life. Shit, the time at the Browns', I swear to fuck was the only time he and I both could sleep through the night. Now it takes pussy or booze, sometimes both, and even then I can only crash for four or five hours before the acid builds up and I have to get up and puke.

My mother was told I had severe acid reflux as a child. The doctor said it would scar my vocal chords if she didn't treat it. The rasp in my voice today is from her neglect. Only, in her mind, it was the evil inside of me bubbling over and spilling out.

I don't know how many times she would make me sleep outside so I wouldn't throw up my vile evil spirits inside her house, releasing them around her precious boy, Waylon.

Going back to Georgia isn't my ideal getaway, but I have to be there to lay to rest the first woman who took me into her heart and home without ever once looking at me like I was evil. George and Doris Brown were the first people to take me and Waylon in and not look at us as either one person or the sides of good and evil. They accepted me as Whitton, they gave me freedoms to draw, to run, to ride my bike down the street. And, in the long run, they gave me the only place I've ever felt at home. In doing so, I was able to be comfortable and be who I wanted to be.

Christmas lights twinkle. They sparkle against the night sky over the arch of the house. Waylon and I helped Mr. George all weekend to get the lights hung and the tree up. Doris and Coley, another foster child, got the tree decorated.

I lay on the front lawn with my hands behind my head as I watch each individual bulb shine. The string only works if each bulb does its job. One fails, they all fail. Sometimes that's how I feel about Waylon and I. If one of us should falter we take us both down.

"Whitton," Ms. Doris calls from the front door, and I raise my hand so she can see I'm in the yard. I start to rise. "Oh, sugar, don't get up," she instructs, and I lay back down.

Within seconds the shadow of her frame comes over me before she stretches out beside me. "Y'all did a great job!"

"It turned out exceptional," I say, knowing it was all Mr. George guiding us.

"Whitton, you see the way the lights get brighter the longer they shine?"

"I'm okay, Ms. Doris, no need to have some life comparison to the lights." I try to quiet the woman beside me who is always trying to give us kids these lessons.

"How many times have Mr. George and I been blessed to have you and Waylon return to us now, Whitton?"

"Six, Ms. Doris."

"How many Christmas' have we had together?"

"Five, Ms. Doris."

"Five of the best Christmas' this house has ever seen." I hear the emotion in her voice. "Mr. George and I, we have this big old house, Whitton, and had a lot of kids come through. You and Waylon are like those lights, the longer we have to see your lights shine, the brighter they get."

"Ms. Doris, don't get all emotional on me. I'm a sixteen-year-old boy, I don't hug and sh– stuff." I stop myself from cussing out of respect for the woman beside me.

She laughs. "Whitton, you will go far."

I huff. Waylon will be the one to make it in life. I'm just along for the ride.

"You know, like the tiny bulbs that hold so much light, you, Whitton, have so much to give the world. You're honest, hardworking, and talented. Believe and you can shine brighter than every light around you."

Ms. Doris didn't let the past define us. She said we were each a blessing and a part of her life to show her the future is full of possibilities. She never once let us use our pasts or where we came from as an excuse not to do our very best. Time would pass, Waylon and I would get shuffled somewhere else. Only, somehow, we would always end up back with the Browns'. They gave us the only solid home we ever had until we found life with Ruthless Rebels. As my mind goes back, I remember Roelyn, too.

"Is there anything you don't do well?" Roelyn asks over my shoulder in art class. We have to draw an abstract piece in charcoal.

"Roe, I think you may have more black soot on you than the paper."

"Possibly," she laughs, and I swear its heaven to my ears.

I continue to smudge out the shadows to the piece.

Roelyn Madeline Duprey always believed in me. There wasn't a single thing she ever doubted I could do. Including breaking her heart.

"The power you have in those eyes, Whitton. It's the kind of power that can break this girl's heart in one glimpse," she whispers as her lips brush against mine, and her deep green pupils pierce into mine.

If only she knew the power she held in her eyes, her hands, her soul, and her heart. Luckily, for me, she didn't, and I didn't stick around long enough for her to realize it.

One thing I learned from Waylon is the pain of losing it all to a woman. The difference between Roe and Waylon's woman was mine had a heart; his, well, it's yet to be determined if she had a soul.

CHAPTER 5

CHALK UP ANOTHER BAD DAY IN THE BOOKS!

Roe

Istep out to the warm Georgia spring time air.

It's early morning so the sun is just starting to come up. I need to get to work because I'm only doing a half day so I can attend the Browns' services, and I need to make sure all my plans are in order for the afternoon.

The emotions are so hard. It's been a few days since the accident, days since I looked in a precious little girl's eyes and fought not to scoop her up and run away with her.

My mom passed away a little over a year ago, my dad left before I could even make a memory with him. I long to have a family. Things before my mom's passing were rocky, to say the least. I've never had the comforts and securities of someone who would really stay. My mom had to work all the time to take care of us. She had boyfriends, all of which came and went. Some, well I can't even let my mind go back to some of them. Those times alone still make the fear rise. Locks, they are the best invention ever. My mom didn't know and then she did. She took my back, she did what a good mother should, that's what matters. My hope is Marlayna gets her locks.

I knew better than to believe in people. Mom did too. The one time I let myself believe someone was with me for the long run, he left and never even glanced back.

Maybe one day.

I make it to my car not really paying attention. Starting the engine, I notice a light on the dashboard I haven't seen before. Knowing I have so much to do, I put the car in reverse and back out of the driveway. I don't make it far before my steering wheel is shaking and the roaring noise I've heard down my road most certainly is coming from my little Toyota Celica.

Tears already threaten to fall because the Browns' were good people and the community will miss them. Getting out to see I have a flat tire, the tears I've been trying to hold in finally spill over.

"Okay, Roe," I tell myself, blowing out a shaky breath. I pop the trunk and pull out the spare tire and tools necessary, clearing my tears.

Once again, I'm fighting back memories. Everything always leads back to him. I hate it. Too much of my past entwines with Whitton, and I feel like I may suffocate under the weight of what could have been.

"Come on, Roe! You can't risk getting stranded after work one night," Whitton explains as we sit in my driveway with my car on a jack.

I recently got my license. I've been working summers and now after school at the local burger joint. Sometimes I don't get off work until after ten, and Whitton says I need to be able to take care of myself just in case. Last week, he taught me about checking the oil, the radiator fluid, antifreeze, and general maintenance problems I may encounter. This week, it's all about changing a tire.

It's miserable.

The lugnuts are on too tight, and I swear I'm going to pull a muscle trying to get them off. Then the tire itself weighs a whole lot more than that little donut I have to put on to replace it. I want to smack myself for buying this car because the chrome rims looked shiny.

They shine alright, and weigh a ton.

Hubcaps are way better, now I know.

Shaking my head, I push away the memory and get to work changing my tire. Whitton rode out of here years ago, he didn't look back. I need not keep looking to the past even in my memories. I just wish he didn't haunt everything.

When I chose my clothes today, it was to pay respect to the Browns'. Now, I'm grateful I chose black for the mere fact I probably have dirt or something on my skirt. Being a preschool teacher, I never wear skirts. The little children are too fast going from one thing to another, and getting up and down off the floor could cause more than one mishap.

I look down to my knees where I bent on the ground. Lucky me, there's a runner in my pantyhose, good thing I shaved. I'll remove them when I get to work.

Pulling into the school, an unsettling feeling hits me like a punch to the gut. This day is already bad, how much worse can it get?

That same question lingers in my head as I look around my classroom at the nineteen very energetic kids. Now, my class is usually hyped up, but it's as if their parents fed them sugar for breakfast with a side of soda. What's worse, I don't have the pick-me-up I normally have.

It didn't help that Ms. Marie came in this morning and said there is still no word on little Marlayna. I just hope she's in a place where she feels safe.

Poor Miss Jennifer is feeling the pinch, and I feel bad. Unfortunately, I'm not sure a mask could change my mood about today. It's like everything has rolled up in one big ball so tight, I'm going to unravel. No matter how much I try to keep it together, even my students can see it.

Johnny comes over to me and puts his hand on my knee. "Don't be sad, Ms. Roe. It's okay." A smile comes to my face. A child's resilience is something I admire greatly.

"I'll be just fine, buddy. Thanks."

I'm able to get through the motions of the morning before taking the afternoon off, and by the time I get to the church, I'm no better. Exiting the car, I see many faces that I know and nod, giving small smiles. Growing up here means knowing a lot of people. Being a teacher in the community means knowing practically everyone.

My smiles aren't as broad and greetings are more demure. Mr. and Mrs. Brown are being laid to rest together. I've never been to a double funeral, and as I enter the church with the many pews filled with people, I'm not liking it much. It's double the grief, but it does make sense. Mr. and Mrs. Brown would have wanted it this way.

I take a seat at the end of a pew about ten rows in. There are about twenty in front of me, but this one didn't have anyone in it. It's not that I don't want to be around people, it's that everyone deals with grief differently and talking and laughing isn't my way.

I know people believe in celebrating their lives. I agree. But I also want to mourn. I need to mourn. I need to find that release of the sadness in their loss.

Looking up to the front, waves of emotions hit me as thoughts of my mother laying up there come back full force. A year, a decade—I'll never get over her loss.

I sob in the front pew trying to be quiet for the pastor to talk, but having a hard time doing so. My mother was my best friend, my confidant. She was all I had and now, she's gone. Poof. One day here, the next day I'm burying her in the ground never to see her or hear her laugh again.

She'd burn the pancakes every Sunday morning and do it with a smile after we came to this exact church. The tears fall as I hold the tissue to my face. My best friend, Elizabeth, puts her arm around me, giving me her strength and I need it. Now, more than ever.

I'm jolted back in to the present by the sound of the pastor's voice and pay attention to everything he says. My grief isn't as strong as when I was here for my mother, but that weight is something I continue to carry daily. To this day, I can't eat non-burnt pancakes.

"Now, Mrs. Cummings would like to say a few words." Inside, I smile just a bit, because knowing Mrs. Cummings, she won't say a few words. She'll have a whole mess of them. I blow out a breath and grab my tissue blotting my eyes.

This is the part where people can talk about the good times, and it usually rises a chuckle from the audience. Me, I just can't feel that in here this time. I want to, but it's like I'm not designed to. This is my grieving time, and laughter will come later. With my mother, it didn't come for months. Grief is a powerful thing. Even when someone's not dead and they leave you, the pain is there.

"George and Doris were outstanding members of the community. They took care of so many children, giving them a safe place to life." My heart constricts first thinking of Marlayna and then Whitton. If it weren't for the Browns', I wouldn't have either one of them in my life. I know it's painful, but they also brought joy. The Browns' gave me more than they ever realized, and it sucks I can't tell them thank you.

"The best part of George and Doris was their love for each other. Married over forty-six years, they were like high schoolers sometimes." She lets out a chuckle, lots of the congregation follows. I do not. "I always said to my Charles that those two are models for all of us. They had so much love to give and gave it freely to everyone, never meeting a stranger. There will be no one like them, and they will be truly missed."

Mrs. Cummings grabs her little papers and moves from the podium and to her seat. She didn't talk nearly as long as I thought she would, but she got out what needed to be said with very few words.

The Browns' had no biological children, but fostered several. As I look around, I remember some faces of those children. Only a few, though. One is crying. Another is staring into space. They have to be in their twenties or so. I've never been in their position and don't deem to know what they're feeling.

That's when I feel it behind me. Eyes, like they are boring into my skull prying for my attention. Unable to stop myself, I turn and stop breathing as complete and utter shock overtake me. Whitton Thorne stares back at me, and I swear time freezes for a moment. No one moves. No one blinks. Nothing exists except the connection with our eyes.

I suck in air coming to a point of pure need. I swear I see Whitton's lip tip just a touch, but the scars on his face hide it well. He always saw himself as damaged, but I never once did. Those scars on the outside meant nothing to me. It was who he was as a person that I loved. The scars just made him unique.

A fresh wave of hurt hits me. He came back for the funeral, but never once thought of coming back for me. I quickly turn in my seat and new tears fall from my eyes. Love wasn't enough for Whitton. At least I thought he loved me, but maybe we were just young and I was stupid and foolish. At least that's the way I feel right now with him sitting behind me and feeling his eyes on the back of my head.

Part of me wants to run away and remove myself from his stare, but I would never disrespect the Browns' like that. All the hurt from my mother, the Browns', and Whitton cascades through me. I bow my head and let the tears freely flow.

I let the emotions pour. For the first time in a long time, I let all the pain consume me. Pain from my losses and for the dreams that will never be a reality.

CHAPTER 6

A WOMAN HOLDS FAR TOO MUCH POWER IN THE DEPTHS OF HER EYES!

Skinny

I shouldn't do it.

I should just pay my respects and ride out of Blakely, Georgia without a second thought.

Only, I can't.

The selfish, gluttonous fucker I am can't be here, see her, and not make my presence known.

I stare. With fervor, fury, and need, I stare at the back of her head full of brown locks. When she turns her head, our eyes lock and I read her.

I read Roelyn Duprey like a book.

She still wants me, she still loves me, and she still, without a doubt, knows when I'm around. She feels me and she feels deep.

I fight back the smile knowing there was a small tip of my lips. I fight my internal cravings to stand from my pew, rows behind her, and slide in pressing my thighs to hers. I fight the piece of me that has always been hers from going up and claiming what I have craved for all of my life.

Her shoulders shake as her emotions win the war she's fighting inside.

Is this emotion for the Browns', for me, or for it all?

Her mother died, and she cried.

I know because I watched. In this very same church, I stood outside and watched through a window. At the cemetery, I was twelve rows over ten rows deep away, but I watched with determination to feel every ounce of her pain, her loss, and take it on as my own.

I didn't stay. No, as soon as it was done, I hit the road back to Bama and no one even knew I was here. Not even Waylon.

I'll do the same today. No one will know but Roe and Waylon that I came here. No one needs to.

Even as my insides crawl and my skin prickles to be near her, I will leave and I won't disrupt her day any more than I already have with my mere presence.

I close my eyes, breaking the bond between us. Giving her the relief to mourn without the weight of my stare on her and giving myself the freedom once again to walk the fuck away.

Silently, I let my mind give the praise, the respect, and the adoration to the two people who gave my brother and me a home, a sense of family, belonging, and a desire to be more than the white trash we were born to be.

As the preacher sets up to say a final prayer, I stand and leave the building. I was able to come inside a church and it didn't burn down.

Take that, Mother! I think as I climb on my Harley parked off to the side of the lot. Slipping the key in, I pause.

"Whitten, you can be anything you want to be in this world. There are so many doors that can open for you," Mrs. Brown says, looking over my math homework. I fucking hate math. Mrs. Brown says it's because it's too easy for me. She's right, but I'll never tell her that.

Ever since Waylon and I moved here, Mrs. Brown has told both of us this same thing. I believe Waylon can be, me—no. It's not in the cards for me.

I say nothing.

"Whitten Thorne. You mark my words. You will find your happy in this world."

Closing my eyes, I suck in the clean air. Mrs. Brown always had high hopes for me, same as Roe. They both saw something in me that wasn't there, but damn there were times I wished it was. Just once— but that's not in my cards.

People begin to exit the church and just before I crank my bike, Roe steps out into the sunlight. Damn, she grew up even more beautiful than the last time I saw her. Her brown hair is pulled together at the nape of her neck. Her skin is creamy.

She looks out into the parking lot. Her eyes connect with mine, and the wind leaves my body. Fuck. Roe's lips part and her chest rises and falls rapidly. The desire in her eyes makes my cock hard. Only Roe would take a look at this mangled face and see something that's not there.

A child's voice comes from somewhere, and Roe's eyes leave me. I follow the sound as a small child with light brown pigtails goes running up to Roe, arms open. A smile beams on Roe's face as she bends down, arms open, and the little girl runs into them. Roe's arms go around her, and her eyes close as if she's the happiest person on the planet.

It could only be one thing, and my gut twists at the thought. The acid inside me churns, and damn the shit burns.

She has a kid. Some lucky motherfucker got to have Roe and start a family with her. He was given a gift. One I only wish I was worthy of, and instantly, I fucking hate the man.

Roe was mine. Mine!

I should have listened to Waylon and stayed away.

Seeing Roe with her daughter, happy, is a punch to the gut that I didn't fucking need. It's just another example of my mother being right. Nothing good will ever happen in my life. Everything I touch will go up in smoke. She marked me, scarred me so I would remember. She wanted everyone to know, to see me for the filth and evil I am so they wouldn't touch me.

My brothers and club are as good as it'll ever get. The one woman who could see beyond the scars—is really gone. I'm no fool, but I guess there was a little bit of hope. Small and I didn't deserve to hold on to it. This just brings it all to a close. Roe's happy, and that's what she deserves.

It's why I left and didn't come back. She needed to move on. It stings, but this is what I wanted, right?

She gave me the gift of knowing what it is for someone to see beyond my marks. She will always own a piece of me. The only thing good in my black heart is tied to Roelyn Duprey. She need not know it. She's got it good, and I'm going to pull out of here and keep it good for her.

I crank my bike and get the fuck out of Blakely, Georgia. I may have to come back, but at least for right now, I can put some distance between myself and the woman who has had my heart and soul for far too long.

CHAPTER 7

THE INNOCENCE OF A CHILD'S ACCEPTANCE IS PURE, HOLD IT TIGHT!

Roe

The little girl in my arms squeals with excitement, and I feel the same. Marlayna is here. I look up at Ms. Marie who beams a smile. She says nothing and allows Marlayna and I to have a moment.

Everything about today is forgotten as I cherish this very second, every second I hold it tight. I fight back the tears as I inhale the sweet scent of her shampoo. Her fingertips are small and soft against my back as she hugs me with all her little strength. We pull away, and her eyes are bright in a way that soothes the ache in my soul.

The strength of this little girl, the maturity in which she faces everything, it both kills me and lifts me up. Kids shouldn't have to know the kind of life Marlayna has. No, adult problems are something I wish no child had to face. Let them be young, be free. There are plenty of problems to assault them in their futures, at least allow them to have a childhood without worry.

I smile down at the little girl who will carry a piece of my soul with her forever even if she doesn't know it.

That's when I hear the sound of a motorcycle roar to life. My head jerks to the side as I watch Whitton once again running away from me. Not that I should be surprised. It's what he does best after all. The pain cuts deep, but not nearly as deep as the last time. This is what he does. I can't control it and gave up trying to understand it a long damn time ago.

"Ms. Roe," Marlayna says, getting my attention. "I brought you something." She smiles sweetly and reaches in her little pocket. Unfolding the crumpled piece of construction paper, she hands it to me.

The design is circles, squares, and hearts of many colors.

"I sleep with your blanket," she tells me proudly. "Since I can't make you a blanket, I drew you one."

Teaching–I wanted to teach to touch the lives of children. I want to be the teacher who leaves a lasting moment of good in each child's life.

"Your blanket is magic. It keeps the bad dreams away. Like the magic carpet that flies, your blanket keeps all the bad away." She points to a circle on the paper, "Like Captain America, you can have a shield too, Ms. Roe."

I smile big back at her. "Captain America, huh? Where did you learn about him?"

"TV!" she says excitedly, like I should already know the answer.

"We have to get an early dinner, if you would like to join us, Roe," Ms. Marie interrupts us. My eyes meet hers trying to understand. "I have to have her back before seven."

It's then I realize, Ms. Marie doesn't get to keep Marlayna. This may be the last moment I have with the precious little girl in front of me.

"Ms. Marie is taking me to a place I can eat as much as I want. They even have an ice cream machine she says," Marlayna explains and puts her small hand in mine. "Come with us, Ms. Roe, you can eat as much as you want too." She pauses, looking to Ms. Marie. "I think," she corrects.

"It's a buffet, sweetie, everyone can eat all they want," Ms. Marie explains.

Her hand is small inside of mine, but the weight of the emotions is what I feel. With Marie leading the way, I let Marlayna take me to her car and I climb in beside her.

Dinner is spent with her eating a little bit of everything, it seems. I commit to memory everything I can from the way she uses her fork to way she dips her carrot sticks in ranch dressing. It's simple, yet the small act means the world.

The ride from the restaurant back to my car is quiet. Goodbye is hard, and I can imagine Marlayna has had more goodbyes than anyone should have in her four years alive.

Marie parks beside my car, and I decide to keep it short and simple.

"Marlayna, thank you for coming to see me today and for letting me go to dinner."

"It was a hard day, Ms. Roe. Ms. Marie told me you grew up with Ms. Doris and Mr. George."

I wrap my arm around her shoulders and pull her close. "It was but you made it so much better, Marlayna."

Her body gives a little shrug. "Thank you for the blanket, Ms. Roe."

"Thank you for the picture, Marlayna," I say, barely managing to keep my emotions at bay.

"I won't be coming back, Ms. Roe." The honesty and innocence of this child is overwhelming.

My heart shatters at her frankness. "We had a good day sweetie," Marie says as she watches us from her rearview mirror, tears filling her eyes.

"Marlayna, I'm always gonna have your picture, and you're always in my heart," I explain as I find the strength to wrap both my arms around her and then slowly pull away.

"You're always in my heart, Ms. Roe," she whispers but doesn't cry.

With every ounce of willpower I can muster, I exit the car and shut the door. If she can be this strong, so can I. As much as this kills me, it's beyond my control and I have to face the facts.

Rather than climb in my car, I stand beside them as Marie backs out and pulls away. I wave as Marlayna turns her little head to look out the back windshield to see me.

One last glance. One last memory. One last moment.

I should get in my car and put an end to this day. I should run, not walk, in hopes that tomorrow the sun will shine brighter. Instead, my feet take me to the doors of the church. Opening the door, not a sound but the creak of my steps echoes the space. The lights still shine as brightly as they did only hours ago when the place was filled with people mourning the Browns'. For some unexplained reason, a sense of calm comes over me. Unfortunately, it only lasts a brief moment because my eyes dart right to the spot where Whitton sat only a few hours again.

Whitton. Even after all this time, that man has this weird power over me. Like some unexplained connection that binds and twists us together in a unique way. I hate that, yet love it at the same time.

I move to sit in the exact spot Whitton vacated, being a glutton for punishment and all. The warmth from his touch is gone, but the remembrance of him, the way his eyes took me in still remains. I had so many hopes and dreams when it came to Whitton and the future. I'd thought he felt the same way, but just like many things in my life, I was wrong.

My head drops, and I stare at my hands laced together at my lap. When will the pain of losing that man go away. He doesn't want me—hell he wants nothing to do with me. Yet, the pain is still there. Like an open wound festering. I need to cap it and move on, but that's so much easier said than done.

"Roelyn," a man's voice says from a few feet away, and I gasp, not realizing anyone was there. As I take in the man, the rush settles because it's Pastor Corbin. A slow smile tips my lips.

"Hello," I greet, rising from my seat to which he holds his hand out and I halt. He comes around and takes a seat next to me.

"It's fantastic to see you. Would be better if it were on a regular basis."

Inside I smile. "I know. Life has a way of getting in the way sometimes."

"Ahh…yes. This is true, young lady, but it is a good thing to have you sitting in the pew on Sunday. Try to make some time for that."

I nod because what else can I do. He is a Pastor, and this is his place. "I'll try."

"You do that. The Browns' thought the world of you. So do most of the people in this town."

My belly warms thinking of my time growing up here. The children I've seen come in and out of my classroom, growing into great kids. It was never my intention to leave a stamp on this town, but I guess that's happening either way I look at it.

"Thank you."

"I know he was here," he says quietly, and my body jolts. "The boy who the Browns' took in with the scars on his face. I saw him while I was standing up there."

"Yes, Whitton was here." I feel my shoulders slump. Maybe coming to church will help to relieve this feeling I have every time I think of him. I've never thought about a higher power or not, I'm indifferent. But if I'm real with myself, I need a higher power or something mystical, magical, or the likes to get Whitton Thorne out of my system.

"That boy had it rough and after seeing him in the back of my church, I'm afraid things didn't get better for him. Don't get me wrong, I hope they did, but that boy has a sadness inside of him that I'm not sure anyone can shine light on."

All I've ever wanted was for Whitton to have happiness. As much as it kills, even if it wasn't with me. Pastor saying this doesn't make me happy one bit. No, it cuts into my soul. Whitton Thorne isn't the man who should be broken like he is. I see inside him, always have. What he could be, the level of love, loyalty, and passion … all the pieces of him he shuts out.

"The way he looked at you, though." His focus goes to the front of the church as I watch his side profile. "For only the briefest of moments, the light in his eyes appeared. It was a flash, something, if I hadn't been so intent on watching him, I'd have missed it. But it was there."

His words should make me feel good. Happy. Excited even. All they do is twist my heart. I really don't want to hear this. I'd much rather wipe it all away. Unfortunately, I'm stuck, which seems to be a lot these days.

"Now, I don't know what your relationship with him is, just know that man cares about you." He says nothing more for a moment, then stands. His eyes meet mine, "I felt it placed on my heart to share with you. Something tells me, Roelyn Duprey, you don't always see what you mean to others and most certainly the man with scars on his body and his soul." Without another word, he walks to the front of the church and disappears, leaving me in the quiet.

"I wish you were right. Too bad you're not. There's no future between Whitton and I," I murmur to myself. Now, I just need to get over it and move on. It's past time.

CHAPTER 8

ACID, FIRE, AND LOVE–THEY ALL BURN FUCKING DEEP!

Skinny

"Whit, I don't know if I can sit like this," my brother says honestly, ready to crawl out of his own skin.

"J.O.B.," I reply as we sit at the diner across from the pawn shop on the end of the main street in our hometown. "Keep shit in perspective, TT. It ain't about the Thorne twins, the trouble we are or were; it's about Rebels. Check the past, brother."

I flick the lighter in my hand and watch the flame. I don't smoke often, but I'm never without a light of some sort. The mugs of coffee in front of us have long since gone cold. Two hours we've sat here, breakfast was decent, but there is no activity at the pawn shop.

Where would LaRoche get the cash to place the kind of order he has without having steady business? It doesn't make sense, and things are not adding straight.

Tossing some bills on the table to accommodate our extended stay, Waylon and I rise and head out to the truck. Trying not to draw the attention of our mark, Waylon and I left our cuts off and our bikes in Alabama. Unless someone sees us with our shirts off, there is no way to know we are Rebels. Our ink, if seen, will let anyone know who we are, but we're making a conscious effort to keep covered.

Transparency.

We need it and luckily, we haven't drawn too much attention in this town. With it being a weekday, most people are at work, hence why we thought pawn boy would be at his. We checked the hours on the door and according to them, he should be open, but not a peep, light on … nothing.

"Let's head around the side. It's lookin' like a long night, brother."

"Fuck!" Waylon barks in the passenger seat. I have to give credit where it's due. He's been toughing it out pretty good. Sure, he's on pins and fucking needles, but he hasn't tried ordering me to hightail it out of here quite yet. It's surprising, but deep down, he knows this is for the club. We'll do anything for them—even suffer.

I pull the truck around the corner about a half a block into a parking lot with several cars. There are no bodies in the cars because they are more than likely in the building working. This gives us good cover, but we're still able to see the comings and goings.

It's around four in the afternoon, so many of these people will be leaving around five-five thirty to go home for the night. We'll stay on our toes to move before that happens.

A week since I've been back here. All it's been is a week since I laid eyes on Roe at the funeral. A week when I found out she had a kid and how happy she looked. At one time, I was going to give her that—kids, a home. Put a damn smile on her face every day. Life didn't have it in the cards for me. Or I didn't let it.

I haven't forgotten a single moment of seeing her, though, and my mouth stayed shut to everyone, including my brother. I sure as hell don't need his shit about any of this. And he's not one to talk, so best I keep it low.

Cars begin to move a bit, but no one pays us much attention as they zoom out of the lot ready to be done with their day.

My attention grabs when a nineties model Toyota Celica pulls up in front of the pawn shop and comes to a rolling stop. Two women sit inside of it smiling and laughing. The driver is none other than my Roe. What the fuck is she doing at a pawn shop?

The woman in the passenger seat turns fully to Roe, wraps a hand around her neck and gives her a quick hug, still smiling the entire time. The woman exits the car, pulls out a set of keys, and opens the front door of the pawn shop then enters. Roe sits for a couple of beats then pulls out of the lot.

"Is that who I think it is, brother?" Waylon asks.

"Yeah."

"Fuck, she turned out good."

Anger spikes. "Shut the fuck up, Waylon." Normally, I call him TT or Triple Threat with it being his club name, but being here among things so damn stuck in the past, his name just falls from my lips. He knows I'd follow him through the gates of hell, and I have. I really don't need his shit about Roe.

Roe drives away, her window down and hair blowing in the breeze, a smile playing on her face. She has no idea, but I've just marked her on my to do list. Whatever she knows about this pawn shop, needs to be my knowledge.

Lights in the building turn on, but only faint ones in the back. The open sign isn't lit up, nor is the front store. Strange.

"Brother, we need to move. People are starting to look."

Sure enough, a couple leaving the parking lot we're in blatantly stares at us as we sit. Fuck. "On it." I crank the truck and pull out. Moving down the ways, we sit and watch. After for fucking ever and nothing happening, we head to the hotel. Not that either of us really wanted to stay the night, but we need to stake out the place tonight. Normally, pawn shops are hopping when the sun goes down. Lots of twisted shit hidden by the veil of nightfall.

We need to be on our game.

I pull and park in the lot. The hotel is a rink dink one, having not been there since I left years ago. Neither of us give a shit.

"I'm gonna get some shut eye. Come get me in a coupla hours, and we can get to work," Waylon says, opens the door, and gets out. He stands there staring at me. "You comin' in?"

"No. I'm headin' over to talk to Roe."

"Brother, you sure you want to do that shit?"

I turn to my brother. "No, I don't. It's the motherfuckin' job, Waylon. I need to know why she's there and what her involvement is."

"You want me to come?"

"No." The one syllable words comes out harsh.

Acid runs through my veins. What is Roe's life like now? I make the drive to her house where I'll see her kid and possibly her man.

I sit in front of her house watching, waiting. What lies behind that door? And the last thing I want to do is cause her any pain. Seeing me, what does it do to her? I read the emotions in her eyes when she saw me in the church. Pain and love.

The thought burns.

Deep.

CHAPTER 9

BASEBALL BATS, FICTIONAL BALLS, AND ME ANSWER THE DOOR TO UNEXPECTED VISITORS!

Roe

Okay, so my door lacks a peep hole. I've never cared before, but my mind, my body, it's all on alert when there is a pounding at the front door just after dinner.

I'm not expecting anyone, and frankly, like the magnet inside the etch-a-sketch my body seems to come alive in reaction to whatever lies on the other side of my front door. No one ever comes over, really. At least not unexpected. As a woman living alone, I'm prepared for whatever lies on the other side.

With my baseball at the ready inside the door leaning against the wall, my fictional balls ready to defend my home, I turn the knob and pull the wooden piece back exposing myself to the unknown.

Shit!

My heart rapidly beats in my chest, a rush assaults my ears. In front of me stands a scarred man with eyes so crystal blue and yet so darkened with the past he lives with it causes me to step back.

Whitton's presence has always consumed me, but the way his shoulders rise and fall as he breathes deep tell me this is as hard for him as it is me.

Yet, I can't help but wonder. "Why are you here?" I whisper.

He steps inside my space; I step back, releasing the door to which he again moves forward to close his escape behind him.

"The kid?" he asks, looking around me.

"Huh?"

Those ice blue eyes come back to mine, and there is a look of agitation in them that I don't understand.

"Your daughter, where is she?"

I back away from him as my body fights wanting to be closer to him. "Whitton, I don't have a daughter. I don't have kids. No one is here but me. I live alone," I admit. "I answered your question, now you answer mine."

I don't get another word out.

Lips crash to mine. His tongue battles and wins its way inside my mouth. I melt.

This isn't the soft, tender kiss of a boy. No, Whitton Thorne is all man, and he's showing me just how much he's grown as he takes command of my mouth.

His hands cup my chin, holding my face just how he wants me as he explores, and I explode inside.

Breaking away, we're both breathless as I stumble back until the only thing holding me up is the unforgiving wall behind me.

"Just as sweet ten years later," he says with a rasp of need in his tone.

Lifting my chin, I say the first thing on my mind. "Just as bitter ten years later."

I watch in fascination as his lips tip into a smile.

With a resolve, I ask again, "Why are you here?"

He doesn't answer, he turns behind him and sees my couch to which he sits in the very middle and extends his arms across the back of.

"Making yourself quite at home, Whitton?" Screw his agitation, mine's what he needs to worry about.

"Don't know shit about being at home, Roe, you know this. Gotta talk, thought it best we do with me here and you there before I find myself up against you, pressing your back into that wall as my cock thrusts so deep inside your pussy you feel me in your throat."

He's brash. He's crude. And I find myself aroused. My panties damp, my nipples hard, and my mind craving more of what he may do to me.

I don't move, but I know my breathing is slow, shallow, and by the way he's watching me, he knows he's got me. Which frustrates the hell out of me. He's always had power and just like before, I let him have it. Dammit!

"Inch by inch, I want to strip those clothes off you and learn the body of the woman in front of me. I want to feel you arch into my face as I eat that pussy like a man on death row having his last fucking meal."

Whitton doesn't move. Confidently, he sits on my couch, legs wide, bent at the knee, and his arms outstretched. The bulge in his jeans tell me he's serious in his desire.

I lick my lips.

"I wonder if you still have that unique blend of sweet and spice. Do you still shave your pussy, leaving your creamy skin exposed with only a thin strip of hair for me to tease? I wonder if you'll explode on my tongue as I suck your clit."

I fight to remain in place while his eyes never leave mine, all the while my blood pressure is skyrocketing.

"I wonder if I can make your body tremor with just my tongue. I wonder if I can make you scream my name so loud, so hard, and so fast you're hoarse the next day."

I'm on fire. He's set me ablaze.

"I remember your taste, the way you loved when I rubbed that pussy, up and down, teasing your entrance with my fingers, but not entering. Up and down, round and round, your skin soft against the rough of my fingertips, slick with your desire leaking out of you, making me want to lick it up."

God, I lean against the wall feeling my body puddle inside—remembering, wanting, and needing.

How can I fight the pull? How can I fight the memories when everything he has said is true? He was a master with his fingers, his tongue, and his mind.

I loved every part of Whitton Thorne. I anticipated his every touch and every conversation. It was more than the sexy body, the bad boy persona. No, Whitton Thorne is the whole package, challenging my mind, my body, and my heart.

Unable to speak, I bite my bottom lip and try desperately to pull myself together from the pieces he's tearing me into.

"I remember working myself inside your tight, slick, heat. Inch by inch, I had to be still or blow my load. So tight, made just for me. When I hit your barrier, I broke through, claiming that piece of you for me."

"Fuck you!" I finally speak.

"Always mine," he whispers.

"No. You gave that up when you left town not giving two shits about me. Now, tell me what you want and leave." My voice doesn't give away the tremble I feel coming over my body. Luckily, it stays at bay.

That damn sexy grin tips up on the side of his face that isn't marred, but I can see the other side trying the same. Scars. His are on the outside, but mine are on the inside, shredding me for so many damn years now. Each look he sends my way only twists them in my gut. Screw him.

He just needs to get on that bike of his and ride off. That's what he does best, after all—leaving. He's a master, and I want no part of any consequences of that.

I've felt them for years, and there's no reason to open old wounds. All those sores will do is cause more pain, and I'm done with it. Whitten, Lance, Marlayna, my mother, Mr. & Mrs. Brown … I'm just done.

"Now, tell me why you're here so you can get out of my house." Even with evened breathing, the fire inside me shines bright.

"You always had that spice underneath the sweet. Glad to see you didn't lose it."

Funny thing is, I had lost it for quite a while. Everything has always been there, it's just Whitton brings it out in heaps.

"Cut the crap. I know you wouldn't come back here if it wasn't something important. Like Mr. and Mrs. Brown's death. That's over; why are you here again?" My feet step me backward and I place my back against the wall, still keeping an eye on Whitton, yet giving myself distance. He's grown up so damn much. Arms sculpted, legs like tree trunks, and a shirt that hangs on him in just the right places. The scars never mattered to me and still don't, but with them he has a deadly air about him. Something deep telling me that he's not the boy who left here ten years ago and he's seen a lot of life and not all of it good.

"Who's the kid?"

My breath skips a beat before I recover. Right, he saw me with Marlayna at the funeral. That moment was both great at seeing her, and horrible at watching Whitton leave.

"She was one of my students."

His hand comes up and he rubs his chin. "Heard you were a teacher. Good job for ya."

"Glad you approve. Now, why are you here?"

"You like that with all your kids?"

I push off the wall and take a step closer. No one ever insinuates that there is something wrong with what I do with and for my students. I've seen the momma tiger come out in many parents, Whitton's about to see mine.

"What I'm like with my students is none of your damn business. Leave." I toss my arm out and point to my door. "Now. Get up and get out of here. I don't care why you're here. Just go."

"I like it."

"Like what? You're a dick. Leave!"

"Can't."

Instead of stomping my foot like one of my students would do, which I'm very, very tempted to do, I look up at the ceiling and think of Pastor Corbin. Where is his divine intervention now? Where are his words to help me in this situation? Whitton doesn't give a shit about me. He obviously wants to have sex with me. But like me? No.

"Whitton, this isn't getting us anywhere, and I need to wind down from my day. Leave."

He rises off the couch. It's so fluid that it looks like a mirage. One moment on the couch, the next only feet in front of me. I ward him off by holding up my hand.

"Oh no you don't." He stops but quirks his brow. "Whitton, this is too much. You don't show up at someone's house and act this way."

"Like what. Like I've been starving for air for ten damn years and have just now been able to breathe."

The world for that moment stops. I swear it. No one moving in the world. No bugs buzzing. No animals roaming. No people talking, breathing, or anything. Time stops. Wow, the feelings racing through me both hurt and feel like happiness rolled in sunshine. Too bad the dark clouds fall over the sun blocking its light.

"Please leave." Pathetic, that's what I sound like. Damn, I hate when my feelings come out. Where's the strong woman of a few minutes ago?

"Can't do that. Now," he presses his body into mine, and I feel the tears sting the backs of my eyes. "I can't." His lips come down on mine for the second time. I try to resist, I really do, but fail miserably. He tastes of the boy I once knew, but so much different, yet still so familiar. I lose myself in him briefly, just feeling. Feeling is what got me into this mess with him in the first place.

I pull back roughly and crack my head on the wall. Dammit, I must have moved at some point and misjudged.

"Are you okay?" His lips are plump, and everything inside of me is screaming to take more of him.

"No, back off. We're not doing this, Whitton."

His hard erection grinds into my stomach, and I gulp.

"Funny, your body is saying yes."

He's got me there, but my words have more power. "Of course, I'm attracted to you, Whitton. We have a history. With history comes feelings. With those feelings come desire … but that's all it is. A way to scratch an itch. Nothing more."

"Bullshit and you know it."

"Keep telling yourself that, Whitton. I'm done. There's no going there again. Now, back off."

He looks deep into my eyes and I could fall into his so easily, but with the force of twenty children on sugar, I don't. I may have had him on my mind for years, but that doesn't mean I'm going to be putty in his hands either.

"You mean it."

"Yeah, back up, Whitton."

He smiles and takes a step back. "Just givin' you a little breathin' room."

Screw that. I move away from the wall feeling trapped, over to the side of the room that opens up into my dining area. This at least gives me some air because it's stifling in this place.

"Either leave or tell me why you're here pounding on my door."

He takes a moment and contemplates his next move. He's always been a thinker even when the people around him didn't think he had a brain. I always knew he had one of the best.

"Who'd you drop off at the pawn shop?"

"How did you know that?"

CHAPTER 10

SHE'S THE MOST BEAUTIFUL FIRE I'VE EVER
SET ABLAZE!

Skinny

One more taste. My cock is painfully straining inside my jeans. My lips want one more taste of hers, but I have to back off.

As much as I can still remember the guttural moans that came from deep inside her as I made her come for the first time, going down this road will be bad for us both.

Since she moved into the kitchen, I follow and take a chair from her dining table and turn it around before I straddle it, giving me a barrier so I can't attack like my body is urging me to do.

"Business has me in town longer than I planned," I give her honestly. She studies me, waiting for more. I don't tell her that a day longer is all, but she'll learn that soon enough.

Roe, always patient with me and always waiting for the next the word, expression, or moment.

"Not gonna get into my business, Roe, but who did you drop off at that pawn shop today?"

With her arms crossed protectively over her chest, she answers. "Marie, the director of the daycare I work at. Her husband owns it."

My instincts scream for me to tell her she doesn't work for Marie anymore. LaRoche doesn't have a handle on his shit if he's calling in the Rebels for guns. Whatever he touches is sure to hit his wife–that's the kind of life I live. No one is safe around me. LaRoche wants in this shit, he's bringing that to his door.

Except now what's at his door could touch Roe.

I'll die before I let that shit happen.

"If you were mine," I begin to tell her she wouldn't be working at that preschool. She raises her hand and stops me.

"Once upon a time, I was yours. For fucking years, Whitton, you had me. Long before you kissed me, long before I gave you my virginity, you had me. And when you rode out of town with your brother, you still had me."

Her words are a physical blow … straight to my heart.

She steps closer to me. So close, if I turned and reach out I could pull her to me. I could breathe her in.

"You had me, Whitton, and I just got me back. I'm not yours, I'm mine. Don't you dare walk in here, think you can kiss me stupid, and stake claim to something I'm not giving up. Did that, felt the pain, I'm good not going there again."

I nod. "What I was going to say, if you were mine, this would be easier. You're not. I can't protect you from the variables in this."

She huffs. "Variables! Whitton Thorne, have you forgotten where you came from? This is Blakely,

Georgia, not a damn thing bad goes on here except, sometimes, a drunk driver. Marie LaRoche and her husband are good people and run a solid business."

"How long you known 'em?" I ask, and she sits in the chair beside me.

Close. Too close. I wish she would have picked the spot across from me. In this proximity, I want to touch her.

"Four years."

"What brought them to Blakely?"

She shrugs her shoulders. "I don't know. I know they are good people and active in the community. Why are you acting like they're criminals?"

"I'm not. I'm simply on a job and that pawn shop is on my radar. Now, you're in that shop, you're on my radar."

"Well, handle your business, whatever the hell it is, and move on"—her eyes meet mine in a determined stare—"and get me off your radar. You get on that motorcycle that's been closer to you than any person every could be and ride the hell out."

"Can't," again I tell her honestly. No way I'll leave until I know everything there is to know about LaRoche, his wife, and if there is even the threat of a paper cut to Roe from them.

"Won't," she counters. "Can't would mean you are somehow physically incapable. Well, way I see it, you found your way back, you can find your way out. You're choosing to stay to handle whatever business you have found here."

"Can't, won't, bottom line, I'm not going anywhere."

I look around the space. It's not large. Tidy, but I wouldn't expect anything else from Roe. She's always wanted everything in its place and for everything to have a place.

"How many rooms you got?"

Her eyes widen, and I feel my lips tip in a smile even as I fight it back.

"You cannot think, for even a split second, you are staying here!"

"Look, babe, I have shit in town that I'm not sure how long it's gonna keep me here. Seein' as you drove your car up to a place on my radar and I ain't sorted what I need to sort yet, it puts you on my radar. Don't know how this all plays out, but I do know I ain't gonna sleep for shit until I figure out a few things and while I'm figurin' that shit out, I'm gonna do it with you on under my thumb as much as possible."

"Whitton!" she roars, standing abruptly. "You are not staying here!"

"Roe, I hate what I did. Inside, I feel that burn, baby, but I had to leave. My brother, he was neck deep in shit he couldn't handle alone. Can't promise you that I won't ride out of here again, but I can't leave, Roe. I can't let something touch you while I'm here. I leave, I do so knowing you're in a safe town with good people so you can leave your mark on those kids freely."

I see her eyes glass over, but not a single tear falls. Thank fuck.

"Whitton, what you felt, feel, it all doesn't matter. The why's, the how's, don't matter. You left. I don't need promises. In fact, Whitton Thorne, I don't need a single fucking thing from you except for you to leave so I can get back to my life in this safe town, with good people, and continue to leave my mark on my kids at school. What I don't need is the man who had all the power to break me to come back and try to have even an ounce of power over me again— whether that's over my heart or my body, it's not yours to have anymore. I have the power and with every bit of it inside me, I want you to leave me."

The passion inside her is on the edge. The fire between us isn't a smoldering pile of ash, but a flickering flame still burning strong.

I stand. Seeing her battle herself, it's not what I came here for. Raising my hands in surrender, I step back.

"I just want to keep you safe. Whatever way I can do that. Know I hurt you bad, Roe." Fuck, I've been hurting. "Please let me take care of you."

"Why do you have to stay here to do it?" The question gives me a bit of hope that she's not going to push me away this time.

"You need some space. I'll let you wrap your mind around the fact that I'm here. Never lied to you, not once, not gonna start now. I got shit to do, but I'll be back. Know I fucked up your trust, but I swear to you this is to protect you." I take in a breath and go for the gusto. "Need a key. Waylon and I'll be back. Can't let anything touch you, Roe. Give me the time to sort this shit and know you're safe."

She nods but doesn't speak. Roe blinks, still fighting her tears but never letting them fall, finally getting me.

"Key?"

"Garden gnome beside the rose bush, lift him and slide the bottom of his feet. Hide-a-key. The spare room is the first door on the right, but it doesn't have a bed. You two can crash on the floor or the couch."

Her expression is pained. The last thing I want is to hurt her any further, but I can't fight my own instinct to know she's okay until I can, at least, sort out what the fuck LaRoche is into.

I take another step back only to find myself take four steps forward to her and press my lips to hers one last time before I turn and walk out of her house, not looking back.

For the first time in my life, I know what it is to feel fear. I'm afraid if I look in her eyes, just one more time, I'll see the emotions between us and I'll never be able to walk away again.

Rebels, Waylon, none of it will matter. I won't look back. I get to the truck and force myself to go back to Waylon so we can scout the shop for a few hours tonight. I have to remain focused and not get lost in my own feelings. We came here to do a job, and we will. Until it's sorted, we'll be at Roe's place when we can. I won't leave her unprotected.

That feeling in the pit of my stomach—fear—it's eating at me inside as I make my way to the hotel Waylon and I are crashing in.

The pull I have to Roe is too much, and it scares the living shit out of me.

86

~

"WENT THAT GOOD, huh?" Waylon asks as I enter the hotel room. The entire ride here my cock has ached. Seeing her again, smelling her, fucking tasting her. Screwed doesn't even cut it. Fuck, I want her to the depths of my blackened soul. Years and one look, one touch—it's just not enough.

"We're stayin' at her place after our stakeout."

He chuckles something he doesn't do often so it catches my attention. "What?"

I don't reply.

"There, what, thirty minutes and got an invite to stay the night?"

"Fuck no. She's got more spine than that."

"Still?" He remembers her well from those days. She was the only person I had in my life, besides my brother, who really meant something. He knew it, I knew it. She was the only good I had in my life. Walking away was for her and for me. She didn't need to get dragged down with the likes of me.

Now, fuck, I don't even know.

"Yeah, same Roe just in an even hotter package than before."

He grunts but doesn't say anything else. The history, my feelings—he knows it all. He's the only one.

"LaRoche's woman was in the car with Roe. She's a director at the school she works at. Roe says they're good people of the community."

He gives another grunt, no doubt remembering the *good standing citizens* we've met throughout our childhood and as Rebels. That title means shit when most of them are worse than the baddest of the bad out in plain sight.

"What else?"

"Other than they run a lucrative business, nothin'. But that means that whatever LaRoche is bringin' to Blakely is going to be at Roe's doorstep because her and Marie, the wife, are tight."

"No one who wants that many guns is good, brother. Just gotta figure out how bad it is. What are ya gonna do if Roe's in over her head?"

"Pull her ass out, put her on the back of my bike, and bring her ass home."

He stretches his arms out. "Good luck with that one, brother. You're gonna fuckin' need it."

CHAPTER 11

WE'RE ALL A LITTLE MAD HERE...

Roe

The water flows down my body doing nothing to cool the burn inside of it. It hasn't lessened even a bit since Whitton left my house. I tried eating, couldn't get much down. Tried working on lesson plans, couldn't concentrate. Popped some damn popcorn and tried a movie, nada.

The damn man comes in, boggles my life, and kisses me. My lips still tingle from the feel of his. They even feel a bit swollen and no matter how much water I put into my mouth, his tasted is seared inside. One face to face visit and my body is screaming to take him. The sad thing is my damn brain is on board with it, too. Which isn't good. At all.

I can't believe I agreed to have him and his brother stay here. I really am a glutton for punishment, just sending out the red carpet and inviting it into my home. He knows where the damn gnome is!

Safe. That word is the only reason I caved. Knowing Whitton, there must be something really going on for him to be in town. One, because I'm here and two, he hates this place. For him to come back. For him to be here, something really has to be wrong, and I don't like that Marie or her husband are caught up in it. They just can't be. His information has to be wrong, right?

Whitton has always made me feel safe. Just before Whitton came to my school, my mom had a boyfriend—a monster of a man. I used to lay awake at night with toys pressed against my bedroom door to make noise. Only when the exhaustion would overcome would I sleep. Thankfully, my mom woke up one night and figured out what was going on. She kicked the monster out. For the longest time, I had to have her sleep with me. Then Whitton came. I saw the scars on him. I also saw the strength inside him. He never once wavered when asked about his face, he was open that his mother did it. If he could sleep at night, get up and push on, well, somehow I knew I could, too.

I shampoo, condition, and rinse my hair, turning the water off and getting out. There are so many questions I have for Whitton, so I dress and make my way to the couch. The news comes on, and my eyes droop. Teaching takes a lot out of a woman. Not only do you worry about your children all day, there's the paperwork, administration, and parents that you deal with. It's exhausting yet rewarding.

I just wish a little girl was still in my class so I could keep my eye on her.

With that closing thought, my eyes fall and I drift to sleep.

"You crash on the couch. I'll put her to bed," a sexy, deep voice says in my dreams. I'm floating up in the air as something holds on to me tightly.

I hear rustling, and warmth comes to the top of my head.

My eyes flutter open and it takes me a minute, but I quickly notice I'm in Whitton's arms being carried through my hallway and into my bedroom.

"What are you doing?" I ask, noting that he has absolutely no trouble carrying me whatsoever.

"Puttin' you to bed, baby." Damn that voice turns me into a puddle of goo. Dammit.

I wiggle out of his arms, or attempt to. He clutches me tighter and I can feel the strength in his arms, which stops me from moving.

"I can walk, ya know," I smart, not wanting to be this close to him, yet wanting to all the same.

"You can? Didn't know that."

A slow laugh catches me off guard. This is the Whitton I remember. The one who made me laugh at the smallest things. The one who took care of me, until he didn't. I missed that. Missed it so much.

He lays me on the bed and I swing my legs off the side, sitting there. "Thanks," I whisper. "Did you lock up?"

"Yeah."

"Okay, I laid out blankets and pillows in the guest room. I'm gonna use the bathroom and go to bed." I move to my attached bathroom and do my business. I even take a little extra time making sure he's well gone before I open the door.

Except when I open the door, Whitton lays in my bed. No shirt on, displaying tattoos that my curiosity wants me to explore. The light blue sheet rests on his abs, which I have to admit have grown incredibly nicely over the years. Looking to the floor, his clothes are in a pile and I note no underwear there. Thank God he's leaving them on, I need him to not show me his package.

"You need to get up and go in the guest bedroom or couch. Now, Whitton," I order, staying by the door, for no other reason except it could be an out, if need be. Never has Whitton been a pushover, so I'm stupid.

"Come to bed. I'm wiped."

He looks nothing but calm, cool, and collected from where I stand. Wiped my ass.

"Couch."

"Waylon's on it, and I'm not sleepin' on the floor." He pulls the sheet over, exposing my side of the bed, and I find it funny he knows this information just from stepping into my room.

"You're not sleeping in here. The deal was the guest bedroom." There is absolutely no way I can lay next to Whitton all night. No way I can feel his heat all night. It's been way too long since I've had a man in my bed. Never did I think Whitton would be in it.

"Not gonna argue. I need shut eye. Get over here and lay down."

Hand cocked on hip, I say, "Don't order me around."

"Sleepin', babe." He closes his eyes, and I debate my options. Oh, who the hell am I kidding. I move to the bed and lay down on the very edge of the mattress. Damn, I'm acting like a child, and I know better than that shit. At least my kids at school would be proud.

The bed shakes a bit like Whitton is laughing. Screw him. I move further on to the bed, still turned on my side so my back is to him. If I don't look then he's not really here invading my space, right? Stupid.

Flipping to my back I look up at the ceiling, then reach over and turn out my bedside lamp.

"Are you going to tell me why you're here, Whitton. The real reason. Why do I need to be kept safe?"

His hands dart out and before I can get my body to fight, he's got my head on his chest and his hand sifting through my hair.

"This isn't a good idea," I tell him honestly.

"We're just sleepin'. You workin' tomorrow?"

"No, it's Saturday. Surely you remember that we don't have school on the weekends."

He chuckles, "Good. Tomorrow, we talk. Tomorrow, we get all this shit out that needs to be. Tonight, we sleep with you here in my arms."

It sounds so wonderful, and I shouldn't comply. But me being me. With the history we have. I shut my eyes and give nothing else. His hand continuously sifts through my hair and lulls me to sleep.

A flood of warmth caresses my body, lovingly. It begins at my feet and makes its way up my legs, tortuously, slowly lighting fire in its wake. Up and down as if someone is using their hands, then their cool lips on my flesh. My eyes won't open, but I don't want them to. It feels too good. All I want to do is feel.

The callouses of fingertips follow the softness of lips down to the crook of my kneecap, stopping and taking its precious time as if I'm the best thing tasted. Heat blooms in my core, sending sharp tingles and an ache in my pussy. Wetness coats me, and I clutch the sheets as the fingers and lips move back up my body.

The cloud I'm floating on is soft, but the more I arch my back, the more coolness hits my skin. Almost like before a rainstorm, only this is my body.

I want the lips on me. "Please," I plead.

"What do you want, baby? Tell me and I'll give it to you," Whitton's voice comes through the cloud, but I still can't open my eyes. Knowing it's him, sends another surge through me as if I'm struck by a thousand different lightning bolts at once.

A strong arm bands around my hips holding me to the soft cloud. The pressure feels really nice even though I want to arch into him and get more of his touches.

"Tell me what you want?"

"Please, touch me. I need..." my words trail off into a breathy moan of frustration. I try to lift my hips, but am stopped once again.

Fingertips slide over my cleft, but there's a barrier and it feels like fabric. Reaching my waist, I begin to pull the restrictive fabric, but strong hands stop me and I growl, letting my feelings be known.

I hear a chuckle, then, "Relax, Roe. I've got you."

My body, tight as a wire, sags to the cloud as warmth comes to my core. It's a mouth breathing hot on to me and teeth that begin nipping the area. Now a finger rolling around my clit, and I want to move. I need to move. It's right there. The orgasm I desperately want is right there. If he'd just move a little to the left.

I let out a guttural cry when he moves farther away from the place I need him to be.

"Whitton!"

He chuckles again. I've missed that sound. Seems like forever since I've heard him. His touches become rougher, taking me to the point of ecstasy then pulling back before I'm able to come. Again and again and again. The coil inside me wants to snap, and it's on the verge if I could just get him to move.

The heat and touches leave, and a weight is next to me. Then the touches come back, but they're light and along my side and hip like I've rolled over on my cloud.

Lips touch mine in a sensuous kiss, and I fight again to open my eyes. It's Whitton, and I don't want to miss any of this. Between that and my lack of orgasm, I may spontaneously combust at any given moment.

"Roe, need you to open your eyes," the lips say against mine, but I don't listen. Instead, I lean forward and take the lips again, my fingers threading through his hair. Damn it's soft.

He breaks away. "Roe."

I attack again, now moving to straddle him. He holds my hips in place, and I can't get to his cock to give me the friction I need to come.

"Roe." This comes out more demanding and almost pained.

Slowly, I open my eyes and gasp when I see myself, noting none of that was a dream. I am, in fact, straddling Whitton, and my body is on fire. He doesn't give me time to say anything. His hand on the back of my head pulls me down to him, and he kisses me. This isn't the one like the dream. No, this is fierce, controlled, and hot as all hell.

My hips begin to move, aching for something to help relieve the buildup. At this, my body is flipped over, Whitton on top of me, his hands roaming my body while mine stay on the sides of his head. So lost in his kisses, I don't register anything but what I'm feeling. His weight on me pressing me into the bed. His soft lips assaulting mine in the most delicious of ways. His breaths tickling my lips as he kisses me. His eyes close as he takes from me and I give.

He's as beautiful as before with many more years on him. I can't tell if the world has been kind to him or not, even this close. Some scars are deep and can't be seen.

I close my eyes and give in. I shouldn't. The rational side of me wants to kick my own ass, but it's Whitton.

It's Whitton.

The boy, now man, I've loved for so many years. My first. My everything for so long. He's here. In my bed with me, and resisting is futile.

One of his hands moves down to my short covered lower half, and he begins to work me again. It's too much, and I have to pull away to gasp his name. It's not enough to put me over, but just enough to keep me on the edge. Shit!

"Whitton!" I cry out, needing more. Needing the release, now.

"What do you want, Roe?" His deep, rough, voice hits me, sending tingles everywhere, only amping up my already alive body. Can't he just be quiet.

"I need to come."

His weight won't allow me to move, and he keeps playing with my pussy. Frustrating man!

"Me too," he whispers. "Inside your pussy."

I groan, feeling myself get wetter. His hand leaves me, and I practically cry out. But quickly it's back, only this time it's underneath my small boy shorts and into my panties. His hands are rougher to the touch and feel deliriously fantastic. His fingers enter me and I'm teetering on that edge, just hoping for that final push to get over.

"Please," I plead.

"You want that, Roe? Me inside this tight cunt? Filling you over and over until you can't take it another second? Coming so hard you scream my name?"

"Yes, please." I do, I want him like I've never wanted anything in my life. I want him to fill me, feel me. I've wanted it for so damn long.

He raises up on his knees and it's then I notice he is full out naked. This long cock jets out from his body. The tip an angry purple. I can't take my eyes off it as he strips my shorts and panties.

He comes back down on me. "No glove," he whispers only an inch from my face, looking down at me. Below, his hips move to find my entrance.

"I'm on the pill. Are you clean?"

"Never gone ungloved except you. Yeah, baby, I'd never do anything to hurt you." At these words, he thrusts inside of me, and I scream from the intrusion of my body. He had to have grown because there is no way he fit inside of me before. I wiggle, adjusting to him as he stays buried to the hilt inside of me.

Whitton waits for me to adjust and when my eyes open, he smiles.

"Kiss me," I tell him, reaching for his face, and pulling him down to me. His hips jerk his cock in and out of me. My body alights and a cry comes from my lips, then I pull him back to me as I ride out the orgasm, feeling him move back and forth. He lights another fire when the last one still had flames.

He doesn't move from kissing me, like he wants to be connected to me in every way possible. I want it, too. I've missed him for so long, and I need to feel again.

Tension builds, higher and higher until I explode and feel him still on top of me as he rips his lips from mine and buries his face in my neck. I suck in breaths rapidly, and my body feels sated.

Too bad my mind just decided to kick into gear now, after this. Shit, now what am I going to do?

CHAPTER 12

OH WHAT A TANGLED WEB WE WEAVE!

Skinny

*R*oelyn Duprey has always been my little taste of heaven. She felt good before. Now, it pains me to think of walking away again. It's a pain, a burn, a bittersweet feeling cutting so deep into my soul it will add another scar to my insides.

I press my lips to her neck, my teeth graze her soft skin as my cock pulses inside her, softening. The aftershocks of her orgasm roll through her one by one as my mind races, and my cock feels at home.

Home.

It's one four letter fucked up word. It's an illusion. A place people tell themselves is safe. I've never been safe at home.

Except with Roe.

She's always been my beacon of light to guide me from the darkness that haunts me inside. She's always been my soft place to land when the wars in my mind wage on and on.

Slowly, I slide out of her and instantly feel disconnected and out of sorts. I lift my head and see the emotions in her eyes.

Love.

Hurt.

Fear.

"Roe," I start, and she trembles under me.

"Don't, Whitton. No promises. No words. Don't speak, don't give me some illusion of what will be. This moment, let it be."

I did this. I hurt her before and now.

"I won't make a promise to you I can't keep, Roe. I'm here. For as long as I'm here, I'm yours. All of me."

She tips her chin up and wraps her hands around my neck. Her fingertips trace the bubbled skin of my scars as she pulls me to her. "Don't speak," she whispers again. I feel her pain. I see the unspoken emotions of her fears. I'll leave again.

My mind goes back.

Tenderly, her fingertips reach out and touch my cheek. The discolored, misshapen mess on my face, she is not afraid of. Instinctively, I draw back.

"Beauty lines inside and out, Whitton Thorne. You are the most glorious man I've ever known, inside and out. From a boy to now, as we get ready to graduate high school and start life, you are a gorgeous, strong, fierce man to love and cherish."

"I'm a mess, Roelyn Duprey, like my face, my body, my soul. It's all damaged, scarred." I cup her face and press my lips to hers. "You're beautiful, inside and out. You're amazing, loyal, strong, fierce, and the one woman in my life I have ever, and will ever, love."

I meant it then and stand behind it now.

"Loved you then," I whisper, pressing my lips to hers. "Only woman in my life I ever have and ever will," I say before deepening the kiss. My tongue meets hers and my cock stirs to life as she moves her legs to wrap around me, and I slide deep in her once again.

"Show me. Stop talking and show me, Whitton," she pants as I slowly glide out of her with the mix of our previous rendezvous lubricating my cock and her pussy.

I didn't come to Blakely, Georgia for her. I didn't leave because of her. The only constant in my entire life has been the passion I have for the woman under me. The only thing I fear in this entire world is the woman under me.

I left for my brother and for her. I wanted her to have a life without the void that is me. Yet, neither of us moved on. How can I pull out of here when the job is done and leave her again?

"Faster," she pants, and I thrust. Hard. Fast. Furious. Passion rules me as I pound into her. She takes everything I give, arching into me, wanting more.

We're both covered in a sheen of sweat as I thrust four more times before she clamps down on me, holding me inside her as she cries out my name. Her orgasm is long, hard, and sends me shooting my own release.

I slide out of her and feel my arms tense, holding my weight off her for so long. Her eyes meet mine, and I crumble inside.

"No talking, Whitton. When you leave, I'll be okay. You'll be okay. Don't ruin this, don't speak."

This time, I do as she requests because the very last thing I want to do is make a promise I can't keep. And she's right, when I leave she'll be okay.

She's stronger now.

She is wrong, I'll never be okay again. Not without her.

Rolling off her, I climb off the bed and stand, extending my hand to her. She takes it, and I lead her to the bathroom where I immediately start a shower for her. I grab a washcloth from on top of the stack of towels she keeps over her toilet and quickly wipe up the mixture of she and I as it trails down her leg. Nothing has ever been more beautiful to me than the sign of us together.

She steps under the spray, and I lean in for one last kiss before giving her, and myself, a timeout. Grabbing another washcloth, I clean up from the sink before stepping into her bedroom. Looking at the clock, it's five in the morning. I go to my bag and slide on jeans and a t-shirt. Commando is my style, the chaffing a reminder I can survive any pain.

As I pull off the bed sheets for Roe, I think of my life. I get up, I go to work, and exist. Everything in my entire world, since I was ten-years-old and met the little girl down the street, I have simply existed. Roelyn makes me feel.

This is dangerous for a man like me.

The shower cuts off, and Roe enters the space. She's covered by a towel. My body screams *home*.

"Don't know where ya keep your sheets, babe."

She walks to her closet with her ass peeking out from the bottom of the small towel. Not now, I tell my cock to tame just as a pounding comes to the bedroom door making Roe jump.

"Gotta roll, brother," Waylon calls out.

"Less than five," I reply, watching Roe take a shirt from the hanger and slide it on to cover her body.

I close the space between us. "I'll be back when I can. Do what it is you do on the weekends, but don't engage LaRoche unless necessary. Don't ask her shit because there may be nothing to this."

"Whatever your job is, it's not my business. Whatever Marie and her husband are into is not my business. Whitton, just go do what you gotta do." There is a sadness to her tone when her eyes meet mine, I see the pain. "So you can go on with your life and me with mine," her last words are a whisper.

Waylon pounds again. "Gotta move, brother, now."

Once again I'm torn between comforting the woman I've always loved and my brother and what we've been tasked to do.

Rather than speak, because there are no words to right the wrongs of the past or promises for the future I can't keep, I place my lips to hers before stepping away and out of her room. As I walk into the living area, it dawns on me—for the first time in years, I didn't start my day throwing up. The acid still burns inside me, but it's not like usual. Even as mixed up as everything is right now, I find this calm I haven't had since I left her years ago.

"You look a mess for a man who has been thoroughly fucked for the last few hours," Waylon observes.

"Shut the fuck up," I growl as we step out of Roe's house and lock the door behind us.

I feel like I have the whole world when I'm with her and somehow it's gonna keep slipping away.

CHAPTER 13

AS IF MY HEART COULDN'T BREAK MORE...

Roe

My body jolts as the front door of my home closes, signaling his departure. While I knew he wouldn't stay, it kills me that he turned and left, once again. Each time he's left, he's taken part of my heart and soul with him.

His words, *loved you then*, thump through my head like a bass drum getting louder and louder. While my words were on the tip of my tongue, I couldn't do it. I couldn't say those words to him. I couldn't put myself out there to be crushed once more. The sad thing is, even without the words, my heart feels like it's shattered into thousands of shards of glass cutting me from the inside out. Like any moment, blood will begin to seep out of my pores and fall to the ground.

That's how much that man means to me.

But me, for him ... he leaves. Every damn time.

Part of me wants to be pissed that he takes off every time his brother does. Part of me wants to hate Waylon for this. Part of me wants to smack Whitton across the head in hopes of making him see. See me.

But all of that does no good. It's Whitton's choice, and he's made it. There isn't much I can do about that, except move on.

How can you hate someone yet love them at the same time? It doesn't seem right, but it's true. All of it. But a lot of that hate is staring back at me in the mirror. With my freshly fucked, plumped lips, face a mix of sated and pain, and hands shaking. I gave myself to him freely. I wanted him, just once more. Once before he was really gone, and it was the stupidest thing I could've done, because now I feel him inside of me.

Not just moving and the ache inside my body from him, but his come. I let him mark me. Hell, I wanted it. Even if it were for a moment—that moment I was his and he was mine. And a moment is all it lasted.

In the aftermath, it was stupid, dumb, idiotic and makes me a total and complete moron. Instead of letting me release him, it's only pulled me closer to him, to the hurt, to the love, to the agonizing pain. And I did it to myself. I'm the only one to blame for these feelings inside of me. Me. And that kills me, too.

I'm smarter than this. At least, I thought I was. Even though having him was amazing, the hollow feeling inside wasn't worth it. It wasn't worth this emptiness inside of me that now wants to invade.

My alarm goes off in my bedroom snapping me out of my thoughts. I make my way inside, turn off the alarm, and stare at the unmade bed. Whitton didn't even want me to have his smell for a few days on my sheets. Instead, he ripped them off, like a Band-Aid leaving a sting, but unlike a Band-Aid—I'm not sure this one will go away as quickly.

I suck in deep, knowing I need to get on with my day. Normally, days off are the bomb and things I put off all week or, hell, the month, got done. Today, I wish we had school. I wish I could go there, see my little ones faces, their smiles, and know that I make a difference in their lives. That I'm wanted in some way, because, right now—I don't feel that. Alone and empty. And I hate this feeling.

After dressing, eating, and doing laundry, I clean. My house doesn't really need it, but it's a coping mechanism that I use well. It gets things done, and I feel as if I've accomplished something, even if I've vacuumed the floors just a few days ago. When I have a task, I focus on it and feel good after I'm done. Not to mention, I pump the music in the house super loud and dance my ass off while doing it.

My mood needs the endorphins, and they come full throttle throughout me. By the time, I'm finished with my house, my smile is firmly in place. Once again the man who was here last night is in the past. Or at least not in the forefront of my thoughts, which is what I need.

My phone pings with a text.

Know you have the day off. Lunch 1230 at Emo's

I smile, needing Elizabeth and her ray of happiness. When I met her at the bar a few days ago, she just knew her man was going to ask her to marry him. I'm hoping like hell she's wanting to show me the ring on her finger.

Be there

I message back, look at the time, and pull my shit together.

The drive isn't long. Emo's is more of an ice cream shop than anything else, but they do have the best chili-cheese dogs ever. The ice cream is just a bonus. Pulling up, I see her car immediately and park next to it. She hops out a beaming smile on her beautiful face. Her shoulder-length dishwater blonde hair is cut into layers that frame that face.

She has on her work attire—black dress pants and a white blouse. She works as an accountant and says the worst part of her job is having to dress up and wear heels. But, today, I notice she has on flats, such a rebel.

Her arms open as she rushes to me, and I wrap my arms around her tiny frame.

"Missed you," she says softly.

"You just saw me a few days ago."

"So," she says, pulling away on a smile. "Look!" She holds out her left hand and sure enough, a gorgeous solitaire round diamond sits on her hand. "He did it!"

I take her hand and inspect her ring as any great friend would do. "It's absolutely beautiful, Elizabeth. I'm so happy for you."

She squeals excitedly. "Come, I need to tell you all about it!"

For the next hour, she does and I couldn't be happier for my best friend, even if a small bit of longing niggles in the back of my head wishing I could have what she does. Even just a sliver of it.

I spend the afternoon doing some retail therapy. Really, I just love the home goods store. You find so much shit you never knew you needed there. Who would have thought I needed a rack to hang my bananas from? And, of course, I needed to have the new placemats for my table along with all the other shit I threw in the cart for good measure. Not to mention I had a coupon for twenty-five percent off, so I call that a win.

After lugging everything into my house, and putting everything where I want it, my stomach starts growling, so I feed it. Nothing too exciting, just leftover chicken and rice from the other night. By the time I crawl into my freshly washed sheets, I'm exhausted and disappointed because the smell of Whitton is totally gone.

But this is a good thing, I tell myself. All I'll ever have with that man is memories.

Turning out the night lamp, sleep takes me over.

A noise wakes me with a start. I listen and hear a few more. Shit, someone's in my house! Just as I'm about to slink from my bed quietly, my door opens and a figure stands here. *Holy shit. This isn't happening.*

"I have a gun, go away," I order in my most teacher authoritative voice I can muster with the shit being scared out of me.

The light flips on and Whitton stands in my doorway. Anger pumps through me, and I grab my half empty water bottle from my nightstand and throw it at him, hitting him in the leg. He doesn't move or flinch.

"What are you doing here?" I screech, getting up from the bed, noting too late that I went to sleep in very small sleep shorts and a tank, again.

"Did you just throw a water bottle at me?"

I cross my arms over my chest. "Yes, and if you don't tell me why the hell you're here right now, you'll get the lamp next."

He bursts out laughing, a sound that I always loved pulling from him, but I don't find this funny one bit.

"Stop laughing and answer me!"

"Babe, our business isn't over and until it is, we're crashing here." He walks into the room and begins to take off his clothes. No, this isn't happening again. Once—I was a fool. Twice, no, not happening.

"No, you need to leave," I order, pointing my finger to the door.

"Not happenin'." He sits on the bed and takes off his boots one at a time and tosses them to the floor.

"You're not hearing me. You are not staying here, Whitton. Last night was it. Get out."

He pays no attention to me and pulls off his shirt. The bottom half of my body responds, and it pisses me off more. *You hate him, remember!*

"Told ya we were stayin' here. May be a few days."

"No, you said last night. No more. Go get a hotel or something. You can't stay here."

Whitton watches me as he unbuttons his jeans and lets them fall to the ground. I suck in a breath because the man has no underwear on. Holy shit. His hard cock bounces, and my belly quivers. Damn him.

"Told you. While I'm here, I'm with you. I'm with you, Waylon's on the couch."

"No, Whitton. I'm not playing around. I need you to go." He can't stay here. I can't do the morning after, bed swipe, and leave thing over and over. No. Each time, he'll take more of me with him, and I can't do it.

He doesn't listen. Instead, he charges me as I step back several steps and hit a wall. Whitton plasters himself against me, then his lips are on mine. I try to resist, but who am I kidding, it's a weak attempt. My lips move with his, and I wrap my arms around his neck as he picks me up with ease.

Our lips devour one another as he presses my back against the wall and his hardness is nestled between the two of us. Thoughts drift away as want and need take over, and I'm lost in Whitton ... again.

CHAPTER 14

BURN BABY BURN!

Skinny

*F*uck, she tastes so damn good. I could kiss her for hours and be the happiest man alive. Sure, my cock inside of her while kissing would be better.

She pulses and throbs for me, telling me she's full of shit. Roe doesn't want me to leave any more than I want to. I didn't think we'd be here another night, but we didn't get enough at the pawn shop and fuck me. Where I am right now, I couldn't be happier. Waylon hates this fucking place, but he didn't balk at staying another day or two. Part of me thinks it's because he sees me after I'm with Roe. The brother he is wanting to put his nose in shit he doesn't need to, but for this, I'll take it.

To have her wrapped around my body, clinging to my shoulders, and devouring my mouth like she can't get enough of me—I'll take it.

Her head has my dick jerking. I toss her to the bed, tear off her shorts and underwear then rip her tank above her breasts. She moans when I latch on to her nipple, squeeze the other hard and plow myself into her, tight, wet heat in one thrust.

Her screams are music to my ears, along with her breathless moans and then gasps for air. She does these, then comes right back to my lips. One of my hands wraps around her hip to her ass, lifting her just a bit as I thrust harder and harder, her pussy starting to quiver from the deep penetration.

Over and over, I bring us there—my lips attached to hers, feeling that connection, feeling all that is my Roe.

When she explodes around me, she breaks away letting out a harsh cry, her back arching along with her neck. Her pussy clenches so hard, I explode inside of her, feeling my come coating her from the inside. Fucking love that shit. Love marking her, even if I can't keep her. At least she knows she's mine. All mine.

We sleep tangled in each other, and the alarm goes off all too soon. She slides out from under my arm as she turns off the clock.

"It's Sunday, why the fuck do you have an alarm set?" I grumble, wanting her tight against me again. For a moment, I feel the acid rising as my mind comes to consciousness. I push it down. I don't want to move. There isn't a damn thing that will have me willing to give up this moment with Roelyn Duprey in my arms again, not even my own fucking body.

I relax.

Roe sighs contentedly beside me.

The acid goes down, and we have this split second where I swear to fuck the world stops. There is no pain, no scars, no past, no future, just this moment— Roe and me. Fucking heaven. All the reasons to believe in a higher power are in this very second because only something stronger than life itself would give me this moment of good once again.

With a kiss to my chest, she pushes off me and I release her, knowing we can't hide away in bed forever.

"Thought about going to church," she says, walking to the bathroom.

I may have made it into the building for the Browns' memorial service, but that doesn't mean I would make it inside a church again. That shit is liable to burn down the second I pull into the parking lot.

Roelyn Duprey wants to go to church.

I need to talk her out of this, except my phone pings with an alert. Quickly looking, I see the text is from Shamus needing an update.

Well, she can go make shit right with Jesus, and Waylon and I can get to work.

Twenty minutes later, I've joined her in the shower, gotten us both off once more, and I'm ready to get to work. I give her a kiss goodbye as Waylon waits in the truck, and we head to the shop.

Surveillance sucks. Anyone who actually does this shit for a living should get a raise.

We put in cameras on both the outside and went and planted a few inside, but the pawn shop and LaRoche haven't made a single move to make us suspicious.

In fact, I don't see how he could afford the order or need the guns.

Bored, I check the app I have tracking Roelyn's phone and see she didn't go to church after all, but to another address. The Browns' house, more specifically.

I feel the fire in my chest.

The burn.

She's gone back to where it all began. I don't want to go back. I want to move forward.

Sending the text, I breathe deep.

Dinner, you and me, six. Be ready.

"You gonna make a real go of this shit, Whitton?" my brother asks from the seat beside me in the truck.

"I don't know what real go of anything is, but I can't leave her like before."

My phone pings, and I smirk at her reply.

Who is this?

Waylon studies me. "Shoulda never called you that morning. I shoulda took off and let you have your life with her."

Whitton. Took your phone and got the number the first night. I send back before looking at Waylon.

"Everything happens for a reason. Good, bad, none of it matters. You needed me, and I'm always there."

I can sense his tension before he finally speaks.

"Took it all from you, Whitt. All my life, I've always been the cause of your pain. Yet, you stand beside me."

I reach over and smack him behind the head. "You haven't caused me an ounce of pain. Our cunt mother was fucking nuts. That's not on you or me."

"Don't want to see you in pain, brother." My mind goes back.

The burn. For an hour, I have bit back the groans.

"Sinner, sinner, you monster!" our mother whispers before the ammonia hits my face.

I learned over the years, that the more I cry out the more she dumps on me.

My eyes burn. I didn't close them tight enough. Fire inside me feels like I'm burning alive.

Liquid hits my cheek.

I inhale.

Bleach.

I blink and more hits my eyes. I can't contain the scream.

Waylon bangs on the door, "Momma, no. Whitton didn't mean to do my homework."

That was my mistake, trying to learn. Waylon went to school, while I stayed home. First grade, he goes everyday. I never leave the house. Mom caught us. I am the demon child, the one she can't let the world see. This is my pain, not his. He needs to leave the door, leave us alone.

My phone pings and takes me out of one of my earliest childhood memories. *I don't know if this is a good idea.*

The fire inside me, from my past, burns bright as I type my reply. I didn't puke this morning. I didn't get it out. I let the peace of Roe soothe me. Now it all threatens to spill out.

Nothing about me is good but you, so everything about this is a good idea.

And it's the damn truth.

117

The day passes with Waylon and I both quietly watching the shop. I know he feels my scars as deep as I do. Twins, or maybe just the shit hand life has dealt us together. Either way, we're connected and always have been.

Past, present, and everything in between, Waylon feels everything I have. Maybe more. We were helpless when we were young. It's a feeling neither of us will survive feeling again.

Only, I find myself helpless when it comes to the way I feel for Roe. She's everything good, and I'm everything tainted.

He drops me off at Roe's place and heads back to the pawn shop. He's going to go in and buy a gun to see if LaRoche is on the up and up with paperwork.

Walking in, Roe is on her couch. She stands and her brown hair comes down in loose curls. Her makeup is done to accentuate her eyes in a way I've never seen on her before. Roelyn Duprey is a knockout without a single bit of makeup, but, with the makeup, I have to fight my cock from getting hard. The royal blue wrap dress has a bow tied under her ample tits making me want to untie it and fuck her right now.

But we need to talk.

So I need to get us out of this house and to a public place.

Sort our shit, talk, and assure her I'm not leaving like before. The time will come I have to go back to my world, my life in Alabama, but I won't simply disappear. She needs to understand the man I am today.

CHAPTER 15

THEN VERSUS NOW ...

Roe

He texted me to go to dinner. This was after I didn't go to church.

Waking up in his arms, smelling him, having him there with me—it was all too much. I needed an escape. I knew he wouldn't go to church with me.

I did plan on going, but passing the Browns' house, I found myself stuck.

Pulling in the driveway, I spent hours sitting there staring at the craftsman style split level home. I was ten when I laid in the grass on their front yard with Whitton beside me.

"The stars twinkle like they are dancing in the night," I whisper to Whitton.

"Do you really think they're dancing? Maybe they're hiding?"

I think for a moment about his statement. "As gorgeous as the night is, why would they want to hide, Whitton?"

He gives a huff. "Roelyn, not everything beautiful is safe and secure. Sometimes the way something looks only hides something dangerous."

"Do you hide behind your scars?" I ask him honestly.

"No, I can't hide them. I just know what it is to wish you couldn't be seen. So, I imagine, if I was a star, I would dim my light to go unnoticed."

Unnoticed. That's how Whitton Thorne lived his life. Over time, I came to learn he didn't hide, but rather didn't stand out. Waylon, well, the more I got close the Whitton, the more I watched as his twin withdrew from the world.

Waylon wanted to hide from everything. He didn't walk the stage during graduation. He played sports, but never attended a single banquet. Waylon Thorne was golden with everything he ever touched or did—only he never wanted anyone to take note.

Even being in my home, he has kept himself practically invisible.

Twins, the two boys are now men and still just the same and so different all together. My mind just reels that they are back here at all.

My heart pounds even thinking of Whitton Thorne. My body still aches for him even after multiple orgasms. How will I survive when he leaves again?

Whitton wants to go to dinner. I don't know what to think, how to react. Every time he gets close to me, my body comes alive. My head screams to get space between us while my body says he is a perfect release.

"Gonna have to take your car. Waylon and I are sharing the truck, and he needs it for work."

I nod my head and pull the keys from my purse. My heart thumps rapidly in my chest. "What exactly do you do?" I ask, feeling like there is so much I don't know about the man in front of me.

"I'm part of a motorcycle club. Ruthless Rebels," he explains as we step out of the house and he locks up. "Keys, Roe?"

I lift them up. "I can drive."

"Roe, I got a cock?"

I nod, trying to follow his macho behavior.

"I drive."

"I don't remember you being so pushy before," I joke with him.

"Man's man, I like to be in control." He smirks, opening the passenger side door for me.

I slide in and he goes to get in the driver's seat. He slides the seat back to accommodate his height. With his right side exposed to me, I study him and can see where he looks so much like Waylon. Strong cheek bones, a fierce jawline, and a perfect edge on his nose.

"Like what you see?" he asks, turning to me and then I am face to face with the other half of Whitton Thorne.

The scarred man with a beautiful soul.

"You are an amazing man, Whitton Thorne."

I give him the truth. To overcome everything he has shows his strength.

He reaches over and squeezes my hand before pulling out of my driveway and down the road.

"I'm far from amazing."

I let out a sigh. Some things never change. He won't accept the way I see him. We pull up to the nicest restaurant in town. It's a small Italian place with soft lighting and great food.

Whitton opens every door for me and keeps his hand at the small of my back, guiding me, protecting me with each step. We are seated in a back corner table. The way the lighting is set up and the dark reds of the carpet and chairs along with the dark of the tables make it seem almost as if we are alone in the space even as we're surrounded by other patrons. The spacing is perfect to have an intimate date with a lover.

It makes me look up from my menu to Whitton. "What are we doing, Whitt?"

"Having dinner," he replies, looking back down to his menu. The waitress comes over before I can peruse the topic further.

I order manicotti and Whitton eggplant parmesan. The waitress leaves, and Whitton looks to me.

"I know you want more. I can't give you more than I am here, Roe. I don't know how to give more. My life," he leans back in the chair as if it pains him. "It's complicated."

"It's dangerous," I correct.

I'm shocked when he leans forward resting his elbows on the table and lacing his hands together to rest his chin on them. "It can be."

"Tell me, Whitton. Tell me why I should have this meal with you, go home, allow you to make love to me again, when we both know you're gonna leave

124

here once again and not look back. How am I supposed to keep doing this to myself?"

He doesn't answer immediately. The hesitation is killing me.

"I don't know, Roe. For once in my life, I don't know. I don't know how to fucking have it all. What I do know, Roelyn Duprey, is you've had me since we were kids. No matter how far away I've always been, physically, mentally, I was with you. I'm always with you."

Mush.

My insides are all melty at his sincerity.

"What are we doing, Whitton?"

He never wavers in his eyes on mine. "Never had a relationship before, Roe."

"And you're not about to start now," I interrupt him as my stomach churns painfully, knowing I won't have the answers I seek. "I remember you telling me the same thing once before."

He moves, and it startles me. With him standing and me sitting, he is massive as he reaches into his back pocket for his wallet.

Flipping it open, he reaches for a worn paper and tosses it to me.

Delicately, as if it's a snake going to strike, I pick up the item in front of me. It's a picture.

Faded, torn, and taped, it's a photograph.

Of me.

In profile, my hair is up in a loose up-do and my face is framed in tendril curls. The color has faded, but my expression is visible.

Longing.

"I took this from the sidewalk in front of your house. You sat in your bedroom window wondering that night if you would indeed be going to prom alone."

I remember. Tears prick the back of my eyelids threatening to spill over.

"I told you I couldn't take you. Told you I'd be there to send you off with your friends, take pics and shit."

I nod, unable to speak.

"Saved up for this piece of shit camera with film all so I could have a full roll of pictures of you for myself. You didn't see me, but I saw you. I saw the desire, the longing in your features from the sidewalk. Immediately, I snapped the picture."

"You took me to prom," I say at a whisper.

"Didn't plan on it, Roe. Saw you in that window, knew what you wanted, and I couldn't be the reason you were left empty on your prom night. So fuckin' beautiful, no reason for you to be longing. Took off to the Browns' and borrowed the suit from Mr. George. Even had him help me with the damn tie. Ms. Doris went outside and made a corsage out of a rosebush from the backyard."

"You showed up," I smile, remembering how shocked I was when he was actually dressed to take me. He was so handsome in his suit, even with the tie a little crooked, I knew I was in love with Whitton Thorne. The kind of love that runs deep.

Soul burning, toe curling, mess up your head because your heart is too far gone to ever turn back kind of love.

"I showed up. I can't deny you." The honesty in his voice, the sincerity in his features, and the passion in his eyes tell me I have as much power over him as he does me.

One question still burns, though. "Then why did you leave me?" I ask just as our food is placed in front of us. I feel the weight of the world as I wait for his answer.

"Had those pictures developed a while after our prom night fun. Got that one, cut it out, tucked it in my wallet. Went to see you."

I nod remembering, he brought me the pictures I ended up taking all night with his camera. I never knew he took this one though.

"I know what happened next, Whitt. I gave you me, all of me, and you left me."

"You laid beside me, peaceful, beautiful. Best fuckin' moment of my fucked up life was right then. For the first time I felt peace, comfort, and happiness. When I left, I expected to come back. Waylon, he needed me. You know he called. He needed back up or he was going to fuck up his whole damn life." He sighs, and I can feel the burden he's lived with all this time.

"Always your brother's keeper," I mutter suddenly, too full of emotions to eat the meal in front of me.

"I looked at that picture before I left. I never wanted to be the one to leave you longing again. I was barely an adult. The Browns' were kind enough to let Waylon and I stay even though we were over eighteen. I had so much shit to sort. My life was a mess, except with you. I couldn't let any of this touch you. I wouldn't let the evil that surrounds me touch you. I wouldn't be the cause of long-term longing. I thought I could leave and you would find someone who would give you smiles, a lifetime of laughter."

"A picture says a thousand words, Whitton. This picture does say longing, but you never asked me what I was thinking when I sat at that window."

"Well," he prompts for me to tell him.

"In that moment, I was ready to conquer the world … with you. I was ready to leave Blakely, Georgia, my family, my friends behind because, Whitton Thorne, I knew you'd never stay here. I knew you were destined for greater things than this small town could give, and I wanted to be by your side when you figured out you aren't evil. You aren't tainted like your mother told you. You may be scarred but there is so much goodness deep in your soul, it couldn't be contained and explodes out of you. Every step you take has always been one where everyone else close to you comes first."

"Loved you then, Roe," he says, stopping me. "Loved you fuckin' with everything."

"Loved you then, Whitton." I pause and look him in the eye. "Thing we gotta sort, though, do you love me now, Whitt?" I raise up my hand. "Food's getting cold."

I don't want him to answer. Not right this moment. I want something more than a fleeting moment, more than a quick response.

I lift the picture and hand it back to him. "I'm not that girl anymore. I'm strong, I'm good on my own.

You need to take your time and ask yourself do you love me now?"

CHAPTER 16

SORTIN' SHIT IS A JOB ALL IT'S OWN!

Skinny

I blink. I blink again.

I wait for the feeling. The churning of my gut. I pause, looking for it, searching for it. The acid is there, but it's not. Roe's brown hair is spread over my chest as she hums slowly, waking up.

Full.

I feel full. Not the normal ready to burst, jump up and puke last night into the toilet. I feel calm, peaceful, and in no rush.

"Fuckin' beautiful," I mutter exactly what comes to mind, watching the sway of her hips as she heads to the bathroom. Dinner went well, considering so much time has passed between us. Another night with her in my arms and me in her bed, another night I'm left wondering if I'm strong enough to leave her again.

The truth is harsh. I'm tough as nails. I can kill without hesitation. Punish without pause. Can I leave Blakely, Georgia again when everything that means anything to me is all that is Roelyn Duprey?

"Good morning, Whitton," she purrs before closing the door, and I have to tell my morning wood it's not sliding into home this morning because there is work to be done.

I hear the shower turn on and make my way out of bed and tug on my jeans. Going out to the living room, I see my brother sitting on the couch already ready to go.

"Coffee is on," he states, looking at his phone. "Reviewing tapes from the camera we secured yesterday."

"You already run?" I ask, knowing if he feels caged he has to get a run in to clear his mind. Being stuck like this is hard for us both, but mostly him.

He nods.

I go to the kitchen and make myself a cup of coffee. Sensing him behind me, I turn around.

"What's on your mind, Waylon?"

"Whitt, you and Roe, this shit something good?"

I sip the hot brew. "The best," I give back honestly.

"I wouldn't blame you for staying."

His words shock me silent.

"Probably shouldn't have called you that morning. Shit woulda been a whole fuck of a lot different."

"Yeah, you'd be running half cocked in life alone. Vengeance is a powerful motivator, but it's also something to make strong men crumble. Not something you can take on by yourself."

"My battle, my war. Not yours, Whitt."

I set the mug down and look him in the eyes. "We came into this world together, and we'll fuckin' leave it together."

132

He tips one side of his mouth up in a half-smile. "Funny the bitch always said you were all the evil. Whitt, you've always been the good."

I shake my head not really sure what to say.

"She gonna ride with us when the time comes?"

"I don't know what comes next, brother."

I wish I had answers, but I don't. Even after our dinner, it's like we are at a standstill. I don't want to take her from her life here, but this is not a place I belong in anymore.

"Need to call Thumper today and sort this shit, though. I'm sure LaRoche is looking for an answer from the club. We've surpassed the original week Thumper had bargained. Don't know that we can push it any further."

Waylon nods just as Roe comes around the corner and into the kitchen.

"Good morning, Waylon," she greets my twin softly while her eyes meet mine, and I read the confusion in them. I don't know how to act either, sweetheart. After all, I've never had a real relationship before. I can say, with every fiber of my being, I do love her just as much as then and even more now. And I want her…

She moves to where I am, and I hand her my coffee mug. "Coffee?"

"In the oven, there's an omelet keeping warm," Waylon surprises us both. "Thought you could use some protein before facing the demons. I mean children."

They both laugh.

"What the hell, Way! I feed my woman, not you!" I give him a hard time.

"Oh, I'm sure you've fed Roelyn plenty that I won't be, but we gotta roll and she needs to eat so she can keep up with all that crazy shit y'all keep doing the minute you're alone together. I'm looking out for you, brother."

He jokes, and Roe's face turns red. I shake my head before I tip her chin up and place a soft kiss to her lips. "We'll be back when we can. Have a good day, baby."

"Okay," she replies softly before turning her head to my brother. "Thanks for the breakfast, Waylon, no one has cooked for me since my momma died. It's nice."

I make a mental note to find time to cook for her before we leave.

The thought cuts me deep and makes my chest ache.

~

THE PAWN SHOP IS DEAD. Hours upon hours we wait and watch to find nothing. Everything we can find on LaRoche makes him clean.

So why the need for a large order of guns?

It's mid-day when we get our answer. Five bikes pull up. Top rocker of their cuts reads, *Black Souls MC*. Insignia is a skeleton reaper. Bottom rocker reads, Live Oak, Florida.

Black Souls motorcycle club was black balled by our club for business alliances five years ago.

"You think they're all rats now?" Waylon asks, studying the men as they enter the place.

"Don't know, brother, but if they have LaRoche buying from us, how do we know it's not a set up?"

I pick up my phone and dial Thumper who answers on the first ring. "Black Souls just entered the shop."

"Got my answers, get your asses home. Club vote came down the minute Black Souls had a rat in their association five years ago, nothing from them touches us. That vote stands even now without another church. They're in LaRoche's business that's his problem, and we got nothing to do with him or them. See ya in a few hours," he orders, and we disconnect.

Any other time I would be more than happy to ride out of here and get back to Alabama and Rebels. How do I leave her?

"I'll head back, give you some time," Waylon says beside me, starting the truck. "Cover your work, your ass, and you do what you need to here, brother. Take me to the rental car place and I'll get something to get me home, you keep the truck. No matter what you decide, I got your back."

If only it was this easy.

CHAPTER 17

THE WHEELS ON THE BUS …

My morning starts pleasant. Waylon can cook. His omelet was the best I've ever had.

We just finished our calendar time and are singing about the wheels on the bus when I hear the distinct sound of motorcycles pulling up outside. Standing, I go to the window to see eight bikers parking and two of them openly armed with handguns on their sides.

Panic fills me.

Not alerting the kids, I make eye contact with Jennifer and continue singing as I go to my desk. Reaching my phone, I do the only thing I can think of.

Trouble at work. Need you now! Please hurry.

The text is sent to Whitton before I can even think twice. The building has a metal roof, and I know my signal isn't strong enough because of the concrete blocks that make up the school to make a call to the police. I can only pray it gets the text out. At this moment, I so wish my room was the first to get the new phone system they're slowly putting in. Unfortunately, it's not.

Marie rushes into my classroom and over to me.

"Take this," she says, handing me a piece of paper. "They're gonna take me. Keep the kids safe, the teachers unaware, and call my husband on that phone number. Tell him I went with the club." Those are the only words she gets out before she rushes out of my door and back to the front area of the school.

I look at my assistant who has worry all over her eyes, but her bright smile to the children gives them no reason for panic.

Still holding my phone in my hand, I move to the side of the window seeing the motorcycles and the men on them not caring, one second, there are children inside these walls that could see their guns. Nowadays, who would be stupid enough to bring a gun anywhere near a school. These guys must have a death wish or just don't care.

Marie strides outside, a wide smile on her face. Words are exchanged with one of the men, and Marie ever so gracefully climbs on the back of the man's bike. There's no struggle. There's no trepidation in her movements. Nothing.

"Ms. Roe?" Jennifer calls my name as I watch all the bikers ride out of the parking lot, Marie not looking back. How in the hell does she know those men?

"It's fine, Ms. Jennifer. I need to step out and make a phone call." The crumpled paper in my hand feels like hot iron as thoughts of what Marie has gotten herself into, let alone her husband.

Ms. Jennifer starts up another song, children smile and laugh as I exit the room and go down the hall to the teachers' lounge. I should call the cops. I should

138

call her husband like she asked, but instead I dial Whitton, my fingers shaking as I push each button.

"Yeah," he answers.

"Whitton, it's Roe."

"What's wrong?" He must hear the uncertainty in my voice, and it sucks he didn't get my text.

"A few seconds ago, a bunch of bikers showed up at the school. They had guns, Whitton. Marie rushed in my room, handed me a piece of paper telling me they were taking her and I needed to call her husband at the number she handed me. She darted out and went to the guys on the bikes like she wasn't scared one bit."

"Fuck," Whitton clips out. "Are you secure in the building?"

"Yes, but they're gone now. Do I call her husband, Whitton? I don't know what the hell to do."

"Are you in your classroom?"

"No, teachers' lounge. I don't have a phone in my room, and my cell won't work."

"Go to your classroom, shut and lock the door if you can. Don't call anyone. I'll be in touch." He disconnects the line before I can say anything else.

Slipping the phone on its cradle, the piece of paper stares back at me beaconing me to call it. Marie's been my friend since I started working here. She's let me lay stuff on her that no one else would want to take. Hell, she's approved to be a foster parent, and they look into all that shit. I can't just let her go and not do as she asked.

Don't call anyone.

Shit. Shit. Shit!

What if Marie's husband can help her? Can get her away from those men? Whitton and Waylon are only two, and they had ten that I could count quickly with them. There's no way they'll be able to do anything about Marie.

Sucking in a deep breath, I pick up the receiver and dial the number. It rings … and rings … and ring, then voicemail picks up. It's a generic message and I know the number for the pawn shop, so I'm not sure whose number this is.

"Hi, this is Roe at the school," I introduce, since I don't know who I've really called. "Marie told me to call this number to tell her husband that she went with the club. Please help her," I plead.

I slam the receiver down on the cradle and stare at it, not feeling any relief from calling that number. Instead, I feel as if I should have listened to Whitton. A feeling in the pit of my gut forms knowing that Whitton is going to be pissed.

I move back to the classroom, putting on my happy, nothing is wrong in the world face on, and go inside. Ms. Jennifer has all of the children playing in centers and a bit of relief goes through me. When they are busy building with blocks, painting or 'cooking' in the house area, they're not paying attention to me or Ms. Jennifer and it gives me a bit to breathe.

"What's going on?" Ms. Jennifer asks as she approaches me.

"I have no idea. We just have to get through the day."

"Where did you go?"

"I called a friend of mine hoping he can help, but really I don't know anything right now. And it's frustrating."

Ms. Jennifer reaches out and squeezes my hand, then we get to work.

It isn't until much later when there is a knock on my now locked door and I look through the small window and see Whitton standing there. Relief and a bit of confusion hits as to how he got into the school, but I race to the door thankful the kids are down for their nap.

Throwing the door open, I launch myself in Whitton's arms, which he wraps around me. "What's going on?" I ask in his neck, breathing him in. Only at that moment do I feel a small bit of reprieve from the emotions swirling around inside of me.

His grip gets tighter, and I hear him give out a long breath. "Not quite sure yet, Roe. Called in my boys," he says this all in my ear softly. "Gonna need you to come with me."

I pull back and look in his eyes. "Why?"

"Because that number you called put you on as a target to whatever this shit is, Roe. I told you not to call anyone." He shakes his head and disappointment comes out clear.

"How did you know?"

"Got ways, babe," is all he gives me, and for some reason I let it go.

"I can't just leave in the middle of the day."

"No choice. You want to stay alive? Keep those kids in there safe?" The thump of my heart gets louder and harder.

"I did that by calling?" Guilt hits me hard. I put all these people in danger because I made a stupid phone call. "I should have listened." The words come out in a whisper.

"Yeah, you should have. Now get your shit so we can get out of here."

"Whitton, I need to talk to the office so they can find someone for me. Go sit at my desk and let me see what I can do."

Whitton pulls my forehead to his lips and gives it a soft kiss. "Hurry."

I take off down the hall deciding to use the 'family emergency' excuse. No one would believe the, 'I just put you all in danger' excuse. Shit.

CHAPTER 18

THEY WILL SOON LEARN, I'M A REBEL!

Skinny

We ride back to Roe's house in the truck, leaving her car behind. I need to get her home safe so I can call the brothers and get some information. Unfortunately, most of them are on the road. I don't know how much I'll get at this point. What I do know is, I'm going to make Roe safe in her damn house.

When the club rides in, I feel relief for the first time since I got Roe's text and then call. Even better, when I look out of her window and see a Prospect driving a truck and pulling a trailer with my Harley and Waylon's. I see my brother in the tiny sedan rental car parked behind the trailer. Climbing out of the car, he stretches before setting his eyes on the bikes. Knowing my brother will offload the bikes, I focus my attention on getting myself ready.

Going to my bag, I slide on my cut, feeling this missing piece of myself again for the first time since we started this surveillance and had to take it off.

How can I keep the life I have in the Rebels and Roe, too?

"Are these your guys?" Roe asks, looking out the window and to her now full driveway. As I peer out, Thumper and Lurch swing off their bikes and make their way to the front door.

I kiss Roe's temple. "They are. You're safe." She lets off a shiver as I pull away and pull open the door.

Thumper takes one look at Roe, then me, and smiles, holding out his hand to Roe. "Thumper, nice to meet ya."

She takes it. "Roe, same."

"Lurch." He holds out his hand, and she shakes it as well greeting him. "Alright, brother. Let's get the run down."

DJ and Shamus introduce themselves as well, before I take the guys out back to give them the run down on the situation. I could tell this irritates Roe, but that's something she's gotta learn. Club business is club business. If she and I really do make a go of this, even if all the variables are against us, she'll need to learn the life. Trust me to take care of her and trust the brothers to do the same.

"Bottom line, we're not sellin'," Thumper decrees. "Now we have a problem with your woman gettin' on radar with these fuckers. Black Souls' are pieces of shit and no tellin' what they're doin' to the woman they've got with them. Did some digging on LaRoche's woman. She's got debt, lots of it, and that'd be our answer for them getting involved with the Souls. Looks like they're in deep, and that's on

144

them. We need to know what you want to do about your girl in there."

"The debt goes way back before LaRoche even came to Blakely," Lurch explains. "My guess, they left Atlanta and used everything they had to build life here."

"Drugs? Gamblin'? What the fuck got some everyday American couple into some deep shit with the Souls?"

"From what Gilly dug up, the woman wanted kids, lots of 'em. Her man's sterile and she ain't got good eggs or some shit in her girlie parts is fucked up. Anyhow, they were doing foster care, got attached to a kid. Spent everything they could to try to keep the kid. In the end, the state took the kid back and the LaRoches' lost their home, cars, and everything and got tied to the Souls," Lurch informs us all.

"The timeline doesn't make sense, why bother them now?"

Gilly takes a drag off his cigarette. "Souls had to clean house after they had so many key players lost to the feds. Finally got their shit sorted, and now they're tryin' to collect old debts. Since it's been so long, LaRoche got comfortable. Too comfortable. Now they called in their marker, looking for LaRoche to buy from us and distribute to them. They didn't think we would see the connection, and it was a way to bypass our rejection."

"The burner phone number Roe called, well, they know her name, where she works, and by now, possibly where she lives."

My heart thumps in my chest because I can't force her to come with me. Well, I could tie her ass to the back of my bike, but a lot of good that'd do me. She loves those kids she works with, and ripping her from them would leave marks on her. But I can't protect her here, while I'm in Blakely. Home for me is with Rebels, and that's in Alabama.

"I'll convince her to ride back with us."

Lurch nods. "We gotta pay LaRoche a visit. Tell him we're not sellin', and he's up shit's creek with the Souls."

"Yep. We'll keep the prospects here with your woman while she packs. Then load her shit and get the fuck out of here when we get back. Roll out in fifteen. I gotta take a leak," Thumper says, moving into the house where I see Roe pacing back and forth, chewing on her nails.

I've got fifteen minutes to get Roe to listen. Fuck.

As I enter the house, Roe comes directly to me. "What's going on?"

I clutch her hand and move her to the bedroom, shutting the door behind us. "You're scaring me more, Whitt. Are you leaving me?"

"Want you to come with me. Pack your important things and come."

Her body stills and I reach for her arms, rubbing them up and down. "You said before you were willing to leave with me when we were young. Now's the time to make good on that."

"I can't just leave now. What about my kids? My job? I can't leave in the middle of the school year and

146

with whatever Marie's gotten herself into. I can't just pick up and take off."

"Know you love your kids. Know you love your job. Know this'll hurt, but whatever Marie has herself into, you're now on radar. I can't keep you safe here. Come home with me and I'll be able to. My brothers will be able to."

"Just like that? Pick up and leave with you, no looking back?"

"My life is in Alabama… I want you there with me. If anything, these last couple of days have proved I don't want to leave you. Now, with the shit storm goin' on and you puttin' your name in there, the best thing is for you to come with me. I'll keep you safe. Protect you with everything I am."

"I have no doubts you'll protect me, Whitt. But what if this doesn't work. What if I leave here and we don't connect like before?"

At this, I press her body to mine, letting her feel how hard my cock is for her. "Never once have I forgotten you. You're the only woman for me to love and cherish, Roe. Have been since we were kids. All these years apart—don't mean shit. I want you the same, if not more, than before. We'll make this work. I swear it."

Tears spring to my girl's eyes, but she fights them back. "You want me to pack now and leave everything behind right this minute?"

"Now, babe. Things are going to get dicey around here. If the Black Souls connect you to me, no telling what they will do. I can't have that, Roe. I can't have that hangin' over my head."

"What if I say no?"

"Then I've gotta figure out how in the hell I'm stayin' with you." The thought of not going back to Granville, Alabama with my brothers eats my gut. The bile rises, and I feel the need to puke. I know exactly how she's feeling and I hate I'm putting this on her plate, but this is life. Hers is worth a fuck of a lot and I'll do what I have to, to protect it.

"You'd do that? Give up the club and Waylon to stay here with me." Her arms come around my waist, and she holds me tight. "Really?"

"Babe, I'll do what I have to do to make sure you're breathin' and by my side. Will I give up the club, fuck no. Just means I'll operate away and have to go back a lot, but I'll figure it out."

"That's your family, Whitt. Can't let you do that," she whispers. "But leaving, I just don't know."

"Gotta decide, Roe. Either you come with me or I've gotta have a serious talk with my club. Either way, we've gotta roll out of here in ten. While I'm gone, I need you to pack everything that's important. Prospect'll load it and when we get back, we're gone. You don't, then I've got more shit on my plate to deal with."

Her head falls to my shoulder as she breathes deep in and out, her chest moving with each intake.

Long moments pass, and I know I need to get my ass out there and moving. "Babe?" I sigh, this kills me. "Need you to believe in me. Need you to know I'm giving you everything."

She looks me in the eyes, and I pray she can read the depths of my emotion. "It's going to be hell trying

148

to find a job, Whitt. Especially leaving in the middle of the year with no notice. I've got enough to float me for a while, but …" She drops her head.

"I've got you."

Her head comes up.

"I've got everything you need, Roe. Know you love workin' with kids. We'll make that happen. In the mean time, no worries about money. I've got plenty."

"Whitt, are we really going to do this?"

"Yeah, Roe. Want you with me. Now and always."

"Okay."

I stare into her eyes, my heart being sewn together, piece by piece, at her words. "Okay?"

"Yeah. I've been alone without you. Love you, Whitt."

"Love you, Roe." I kiss her long and deep. "Pack. I'll be back in an hour. Prospect will help you and load your shit in the truck. If it doesn't mean shit, don't take it. It does, put it in. Got me?"

"Yeah."

I kiss her again, so fucking happy she chose to come with me. Fuck, I've missed her. There's an excitement inside me. My pulse quickens, and the acid calms as I start to think about having Roe at home with me.

I pull away, and she squeezes my arm. "Whitton?" Her eyes blaze with so many emotions. "There's a little girl, Marlayna. She's in foster care. The Browns'..." The pain fills her features mentioning the girl and the best people I've ever known. "Marie had some visitation with her. We gotta keep her safe, Whitton. I can't have anything happen to her."

"Text me everything you got on her, I'll get a man on it." I don't know much about what Marie had going, but I know the state is so short on foster parents that if she was still current on her certification, they might have been considering having that girl stay with them. If that's the case, she may very well be on the Souls radar, too.

"Just like that?" Her eyes light up.

"Yeah, she means something to you, you mean everything to me, so she means something to Rebels. This is how my life works, Roe. Ride with me, and you're gonna see it. Family in the best possible fuckin' way ever."

I kiss her quickly again before I have to walk away and get to work. The sooner this shit is handled, the faster we ride out and I have Roe with me on the back of my bike.

The ride to LaRoche's place isn't long, which puts me even more on edge on how close this shit is going on with Roe right here in the thick of it.

We ride right up and park. Walking in the pawn shop, it's like every other day we've been here. Dead.

No patrons, but the door is unlocked. Stupid.

Vincent LaRoche comes from the back, and his face pales as he sees the six of us standing in front of his counter.

Thumper leans over, resting both elbows on the wooden top in front of him. "Answer's no, LaRoche."

"You can't do this to me," the man's voice cracks.

"Oh, but I can and I did. You got ties to Black Souls. Nothing with them ever touches my club."

We all flank Thumper on each side.

"My wife, they have my wife."

"Not my problem," Thumper gives him honestly. "Came to tell ya, we aren't supplyin' a damn thing to you."

"They'll kill her."

Lurch grabs his side piece and slams the butt of the gun down on LaRoche's hand. "Fuckin' told your ass we aren't into doing third party shit. We sell to you, it's for you—not to be redistributed by some fucked up mess of a club with rats."

The man bites back his pain.

"No feds involved. They put Banger in the ground after they were taken down."

"You think I give a fuck? Feds gone, rats gone, none of that shit matters. Their club fucked their own shit up. Didn't clear motherfuckers the right way. Too much heat. That's not how we roll." Lurch puts the gun away while the man drops his hand to his side.

"No further contact, we let you live," Thumper says before we start to back away.

"My wife," he pleads. "The kids she loves. Marlayna," he whispers, and my heart stops. Fuck.

"Where's the fuckin' kid?" I bark out as my brothers look at me.

"She's at a group home, but we're supposed to get her in a week. To live with us." Bile rises in my stomach, and I fight it back.

"What home?"

He hesitates and I pull my gun, aiming it at him. "What fuckin' home?"

"Keensaw, the group home there," he responds quickly.

"You don't exist for that little girl anymore. You hear me?"

"That little girl is everything to Marie," he whines, and I want to knock him the fuck out.

"And she's not fuckin' here, now is she?" TT responds as I put my gun away.

"You done?" Lurch asks, and I nod. "No contact with the Rebels. No contact with that little girl. Nothing. And you live. You don't, I'll put the bullet in your head myself."

With that, we leave, get on our bikes, and Lurch and Thumper lead us to a nearby park where we stop.

"Kid?" Thumper asks as I walk closer to him, TT on my heels.

"She means somethin' to Roe. Don't have all the details on her, but if what LaRoche says is true and the kid was comin' to live with them, means she ain't got anyone."

"Fuck," TT says, pulling out a cigarette and lighting it.

"Yeah, brother. Kid lived with the Browns'."

"You're fuckin' shittin' me."

I look at my brother, pain and anger warring in is expression. Fucking hate that for him. Tried for years to take on that shit so he didn't feel it. I still don't want him to, but I have Roe now and this kid who means a lot to my woman. I remember Roe's face light up with the kid came to the funeral. That's why I

152

thought the little girl was her daughter. That connection between the two of them, the way the little kid ran into Roe's arms…I didn't miss a beat of it.

"Yeah, makes this kid my business. Therefore, our business."

Lurch watches TT and myself. "Know you two had a rough start at things. Know the Browns' took you in. This means something to Roe—we're in."

This I had no doubts, but I do have them where it concerns getting the little girl or, at least, making sure she's safe. Remembering my time in foster care and all the questions I was asked over and over again float through my head, even though I tried for years to block them out. The main question they asked was about family. They always wanted to know if there were some kind of extended family somewhere that would take Waylon and me in. We had no one because our mother was a lunatic.

The thing with Waylon and my records is—there is one from the time we entered into foster care. Sure that shit is supposedly sealed, but nothing is truly sealed. I have a guy who could access anything I wanted at any time. So this leaves Waylon and I out for family.

"We need to have someone at the club be her extended family. It'll take some computer adjustments, but it can work," I tell them as TT looks at me.

"Can't be us, brother," he says, and I read his pained expression. "We got too long of a history. They'll know."

"Know that." I look at my brothers. "We need either one of you or your ol' ladies to have a tie somewhere."

"Drea," Shamus says without a blink of an eye. "It'll work, too, because she can't have kids and wants 'em."

"She be good at lyin' flat out, brother. Know she's your ol' lady, but this is serious and she's gotta keep a clear head while she answers stuff. You don't think that she can handle it, we don't need to use her." Drea suffered a brain injury while on assignment as a reporter. She has some issues with fibers of her brain that came detached during an explosion. One where she's lucky to be alive.

"Yeah, doc's even suggested we do adoption, and we've already filled out most of the paperwork. I'm sure we could get approved for foster care pretty easily, and I know a guy there."

Damn, this works. I look at TT and ask, "Thoughts?"

"If I can get to my computer, I'm sure I could make it work. They'll want to interview you and Drea, Shamus." Shamus nods like he's already been going through this anyway so it's no skin off his teeth. "You know, if I can swing the link, they'll give the kid to them fairly quickly just to get her out of the home."

I only nod, remembering how often we were moved from place to place only for those not to work and move to another. We spent time in the homes, too, and they were shit.

"We need to ride out and get home. What do we do about the kid until then?" Thumper asks me. Fuck if I know. What I'd like to do is snatch the kid up and take her with Roe and me, but that'll just cause a lot of shit we don't need coming down on us.

"Man on her. Prospect for now. If she's staying in the home, then she'll only go from school to there—if they're sending her."

Thumper nods, pulling out his phone and making a call.

TT nudges my arm. "We'll make this work, brother. Fuckin' swear it."

CHAPTER 19

HOME SWEET HOME ... IN A ROOM – IS THIS HOW HIS LIFE REALLY IS?

Roe

The ride to Granville isn't too bad and with Whitton driving, it made it better. He and his brother loaded up their bikes. Waylon drove the truck and Whitton, my car. We followed in an entourage all the way to the clubhouse. Whitton decided to tell me, when we were halfway there, that he lived at the clubhouse. Therefore, that's where we'd live, too.

He also informed me about Marlayna, and I can't help but worry about the little girl. I know Whitton wants to keep me safe, but every instinct I have in my bones wants me to keep Marlayna safe.

I called work, talking to Marie's boss telling him I had a family emergency and needed to be gone for a while. He asked how long, and I told him the rest of the school year. He did not take kindly to this. I could have told him a few weeks or a month, but once the decision was made to come here with Whitton, I knew I wouldn't be going back. As much as I love my kids and my life there, Whitton has always been home to me. No matter the distance, he's always been it for me. Will always be.

As I stand in his room, looking around, it's seriously bare.

It breaks my heart that Whitt has lived like this for years. There are no pictures anywhere. There are no memories on shelves. Everything is sparse, as if he didn't want to get attached to anything because it would be gone in a moment's notice. This breaks my heart. I never wanted that for Whitton. No matter how much I hated what he'd done, how he'd left me without another thought, I never wanted him to feel this. He does have brothers, and I can tell they care about him.

That's one good thing in this mess. He found a family he can count on, and I can't help but wonder where I fit into this mix. He's told me that I can slide right into his life, but what if that's not true? What if he's wrong and I don't? I could never ask him to leave his family. I never would.

"You're thinkin' awfully hard there, Roe," Whitt says, coming out of the bathroom.

"Just wrapping my head around the last twenty-four hours. It's a lot to take in."

His arms wrap around me, and a sense of security drapes over me like a cloth keeping me warm.

"Know that, babe. Gotta know the Rebels and I'll take care of it."

"Do you really think the plan for Marlayna will work?" Whitton told me on the drive about their plan. When I asked, *don't they keep records of all that?* He responded with, *don't worry about 'all that'.* Not giving me any real answers. At first I thought to argue with him and pull out more information, but then realized that wouldn't get me anywhere with Whitton. Back when we were kids, maybe, but now, the man he's become—I can tell he's not easily swayed. So, I let it go and put my trust in him … and his club.

"Yeah, I do. We'll get all this shit ironed out in a coupla days." His confidence makes me believe it. I roll to my tiptoes and place a kiss on his lips. The kiss turns hot immediately and before I can breathe, Whitton has squeezed three orgasms from me and I pass out.

~

"HI, I'm Kenderly!" A very happy woman with long honey colored hair braided down her back comes up to me holding out her hand. I take it smiling back.

"Roe."

"Kenie, he's squirmin'." DJ, one of Whitton's brothers, comes up with a beautiful baby boy in his arms handing him over to Kenderly.

"You know you're going to have to get over this," she huffs, taking the little bundle and looking down at him. "Daddy just thinks he's gonna drop you or something." She smiles bright. "He's superman, though. He'd never drop you."

"Kenie," DJ warns.

She waves him off. "Let me chat with, Roe." He makes his way over to a set of tables where some of the guys are sitting, including Whitton and Waylon. Waylon, who, by the way, hasn't said much to me, and I need to find out if I pissed him off or something.

"Are you hangin' in there? Don't know the whole story, but DJ told me the bits he could. One thing you have to get used to around here is them talkin' and not tellin' ya what's goin' on. But that just means we can do the same."

"Heard that!" DJ yells from across the room.

"Good!" she fires back.

"Give me that baby!" A beautiful woman with mahogany hair comes barreling through the door with Shamus right behind her. This must be Drea.

"Yeah, yeah," Kenderly says, lovingly handing the baby over.

"Drea, this is Roe."

Only when my name is said does she look up, her eyes warming. "Hey, hun. I'm Drea, nice to meet you."

"Thank you so much for what you're doing. Marlayna means a lot to me, and I just want her to be safe," I ramble, not sure how much she knows, but feeling like I need to say thank you with every breath I can.

"Hun, I'm happy too. Pretty damn excited, actually." This brings me joy. "Shamus and the boys'll get it all wrapped up. That little girl will be here before you know it."

"I hope you're right," I grumble as Kenderly places her hand on my shoulder.

"Trust your man. You know the one who hasn't taken his eyes off you the entire time we've been standing here, afraid you're going to disappear." My eyes widen. "Yeah, that one. Trust your man to handle it."

We spend the rest of the day getting to know each other and when Drea wasn't hogging the baby, I was.

∼

"WE GOTTA go pick out a place, Roe," Whitton says from the doorway as I look at his books. I was wrong about him not having any possessions. He has several books, and I bet he's read every single one of them. He always loved to read when he was a kid. I'm happy he still finds comfort in it.

"You sure you want to live with me, Whitton Thorne?" I tease.

He stalks to me, wrapping his strong arms around me. "Never wanted something so damn bad in my life, Roe. You're it for me, always have been. Know I fucked up leavin' you, and I won't do that shit ever again. Know what it's like livin' without you for far too many years. Not doin' that again. Not doin' that ever."

"I love you," I whisper as his lips crash down on mine. Damn, I love this man, and I show him just how much I do.

∼

"I'M SCARED FOR MARIE. Have you heard anything?" I ask Whitton as we lay in bed later that night.

"Nope and I probably won't. She's not our problem and since she brought her problem to your doorstep, she's not yours either."

"I know, I just can't help but wonder if she's okay. If those guys are hurting her or if Vincent, her

161

husband, was able to get her back from them. She's been my friend for a lot of years, Whitton."

I rake my fingernails over his chest, his muscles giving little jumps with each touch.

"Some friends are worth givin' your all to. Others that bring you trouble, you need to scrape off. Sure, Marie was good at one time, but babe, she's runnin' a dangerous game and involved with some seriously fucked up people. Gotta get shot of that or else they'll be knockin' on your doorstep, and that shit ain't happen."

He's right, and I don't like it. "I know."

"But you still worry." His hand traces circles on my naked back as my ear is against his chest listening to the thump of it.

"Yeah."

"Love that you care so much, Roe. Love that you give that to me not askin' for a damn thing in return. Love that your heart is so damn big that, one day, our kids will have nothin' but love." My breath catches. "But for your safety, our safety, and the safety of our future, gotta cut her loose."

My heart expands. "I'll try."

"All I can ask."

"Yeah."

"Love you, Whitton."

"Love you, too. Night. Get some sleep."

I let it overcome me.

CHAPTER 20

BUBBLE, BUBBLE, TOIL AND TROUBLE, I JUST WANT IT ALL TO END.

TWO WEEKS LATER

"*D*on't be pissed," TT starts out the conversation, pissing me off.

"You know whenever you start shit like that it already pisses me off, so spill it."

My brother pulls over the computer. "Got everything in line for Shamus and Drea to get the kid. Even got the paperwork expedited and just waitin' on the head man, Mr. Sanders, to sign off on it. He's gettin' a call from my guy there to have it done in the next few hours."

"None of this shit sounds bad, TT."

"The woman, Marie, hasn't gone back to work. LaRoche was found dead outside of his pawn shop late last night. Beat to hell, then a bullet to his head."

"Brother," I warn. While I get that the man's death is news we should know, it's not something that would piss me off. May hurt my woman, but not me. One more dumb fucker off the planet as far as I can tell.

"Got a man close to the Souls." This is a surprise. "There's chatter about the little girl being a key to the Rebels. I'm thinkin' we need to ride and be prepared to get the girl as soon as the asshole signs the papers. Don't think they're stupid enough to hit at the home because too many witnesses, but outside of it—pretty sure they're gonna hit."

"Fuck. You tell Thumper?"

"Headin' there now," he says, and I step in stride beside him. TT and I will tell him together. He's always had my back, and I will always have his.

Two hours later, we're on the road back to Blakely. Shamus driving his Tahoe with Drea, Roe and myself. DJ, Thumper, Lurch and TT are on their bikes, and a couple of the prospects are driving the van just in case we need more firepower than we can store on us. Hate that we have to leave the safety of our clubhouse, but we need to get the girl and get home. If we have to take out the Souls in the process, then so be it.

Hated having to bring Roe and Drea with us, but they are vital on getting the girl and allowing her to feel safe. Roe especially. It makes me even more on guard than normal.

It's been two weeks since we've been back to Blakely. We have to drive through it to get to Keensaw where Marlayna is. Roe and I still haven't decided on a home, so the clubhouse is where we're living, which doesn't bother me, but I can tell it's getting to Roe so it'll need to be fixed once we get back.

I'm alert once we're about fifty miles out, or I should say more on alert, watching and anticipating. The Souls are pieces of shit and I have no doubt they'll play dirty, but not at the risk of causing undo attention. But they will try to get what they want, namely us, after we get the kid. How they figured out when we were going is beyond me. Only thing I can think is, just like Triple Threat, they have an insider.

For this reason, we have a plan. One that the women don't know because we're hoping it doesn't come to it, but chances are it will. We have another Tahoe, exactly the same as Shamus' meeting us up there from a fellow club, the Ravage MC. We're on good terms with them and they owed us a marker. We called it in. If we have to do a swap to get the kid and women out, we'll do it. Not only that, but Ravage are bringing in their men to help make sure the Souls don't get far. They are a tight club that have run most of Georgia for decades. Third generation type of club rising now. Good men and even better to have support in unfamiliar territories.

Hopefully, everything will go as planned and if some of the Souls lose their life, so fucking be it.

We're in the SUV when Shamus' cell rings. He looks at the caller ID. "It's the home."

Roe tenses beside me, and I wrap her in my arms as we listen to Shamus talk.

"We got her. She'll be ready in an hour," Shamus says, looking over at Drea who smiles excitedly.

I hop on my phone, sending out a text to the guys. One thing about technology is the bikes have screens on them to show the text when it pops up. It comes in seriously handy in times like these.

Nervous energy fills me. I read Marlayna's file. The little girl has seen far too much and been dealt the worst of the worst in her short life. Her neck and chest are scarred in burns where a boyfriend of her mother's poured gasoline on her and lit a cigarette, watching her little body, at two-years-old, warp, melt, and fall away before her mother heard her screams and smothered the fire out.

She spent four months in a burn center healing and still has scars.

Closing my eyes, I think to myself. Marlayna, your body may be scarred, but I promise you with everything I know in this world, Roelyn Duprey will keep you from permanently scarring your heart. I give my vow to the little girl I have yet to see. I will give my life and all that I have to make sure you feel no physical pain like you have endured before. This is going to be your new life, your new home, your family—all with the Rebels, me, and Roelyn Duprey.

Legally, she will be fostered to be adopted by Shamus and Drea. I understand the setup. But Roe and I will be the best aunt and uncle that little girl will ever know. Since we haven't found a place yet, Roe and I will be staying with Shamus and Drea for a few days to help Marlayna adjust. We have a plan.

The only thing we need is to get to Keensaw, Georgia, pick up Marlayna, and get back to Granville with her.

Just outside of Keensaw, Ravage MC pulls up near us. They keep enough distance that they will be able to stay separated if someone is watching, but close enough we can make a switch to confuse someone if necessary.

Pulling up to the home, we are behind a closed gate and I take a moment to breathe.

Roe and I stay in the car waiting for Shamus and Drea to bring Marlayna out. As to not cause any suspicion, we didn't want Marlayna to see Roe and react.

"Thank you, Whitton," she whispers, resting her head on my shoulder.

"There isn't anything I wouldn't do for you, Roe, and her," I tell her honestly.

She sighs peacefully. "Maybe when things calm down, we can one day foster and adopt for ourselves."

"Baby, you want it, you got it."

She lifts her head and smiles at me. "Whitton, we have a long way to go. You make everything sound so easy."

I tip her chin, press my lips to her. "I got you. Everything else, you want it, you got it. We're gonna get a house with a big yard, gonna put a ring on your finger, and give you my name. You wanna adopt, we adopt. You want me to put a baby in your belly, give you that, too."

"Loved you then, Whitton Thorne," her voice is soft. "Think I love you more, now."

Fuck. She makes me rock hard.

Before I can say anything, we see little Marlayna walking out with a pillowcase of her things and a Barbie blanket in her hand. Roe jumps up to move, and I hold her in place in the third row of seats of the SUV. "Can't be seen, baby," I remind her, and she stills.

To see the emotion in her, the way she drinks in every move of this little girl, I can't help but remember the way she used to study my every move, too. It was like she was always so afraid of losing me, she had to memorize it all.

CHAPTER 21

BE STILL MY HEART, SHE'S HERE AND IT'S GOING TO BE OKAY!

Roe

*M*arlayna climbs in the car, her face is locked tight. No emotions, no fear, just a little girl shuffling along like she's done too many times before. Drea slides in the SUV with her hand in Marlayna's, while Shamus climbs in the driver seat.

Finally, Marlayna turns her tiny head, and her eyes meet mine.

The world stops.

I smile as I see the comfort hit her features. Her cheeks relax, and a smile forms on her tiny lips. "Ms. Roe!"

Reaching my hand over the seat, I give her shoulder a squeeze. "Marlayna, these are my friends," I explain. "Drea and her husband are going to take you home."

She frowns. "Can I come with you, Ms. Roe?"

How I wish she could. The fact is I don't have my certification, and there is too much red tape. Having her be with Shamus and Drea is the closest thing to having her with me. I've spent time with the Rebels and their women. It's a real family and more than Marlayna has ever had before.

"Well, I just moved to Alabama with my," I pause, what do I call him. Looking at Whitton, I watch his lip tip into a small smile.

"Fiancé," he chimes and I want to roll my eyes, but instead I just smile. Apparently, with these men, they say it and it's going to happen. That's what Kenderly said happened with her and DJ, anyway.

"Oh, Ms. Roe, you're gonna get married and wear a dress!" Marlayna is so excited.

"Whitton," I point to the man beside me. "He and I will be staying with you at your new home for a bit."

"Does it hurt?" she asks Whitton, no longer looking at me or concerning herself with being separated again. Instead, her focus is on Whitton. My stomach churns. Not because she asked about his scars, but because of what could come out of her little mouth about her own. I hate that she's been put through anything that's caused her pain.

"My scars?" he asks her back, to which she nods. "Not anymore." He gives my hand a reassuring squeeze.

"Mine do sometimes," she whispers.

"One day, Marlayna, they'll be a part of the past, a faint mark and a faint memory of a time you will look back on and say it made you strong," Whitton explains, and my heart feels like it may explode with emotions.

"Don't worry, Marlayna, his ugly mug needs the scars to keep him from scaring Ms. Roe away," Shamus jokes, to which Drea pinches him in the back of the arm.

"Shamus," she chastises, "Skinny is a good man."

Marlayna has a look of confusion.

"Shamus is also known as Austin, Marlayna," Whitton explains. "We're in a club and we all have nicknames. I'm Skinny."

"Why can't they just call you by your names?"

"Well, we just have these names with our brothers. You can call me Whitton and him Austin, or Shamus and Skinny. We answer to either."

Shamus starts to back out of the parking spot. "Buckle up."

Leaning back in my seat and watching as Drea secures Marlayna in the booster car seat and shoulder belt, I buckle as well.

Turning to Whitton, I whisper, "Why do they call you Skinny?

He leans into my ear. "I like curvy women."

"And I'm thankful for this."

"At a party once, this woman kept hitting on me, but she was as skinny as a rail. I told her I'd break her like a twig. Guys caught wind of it and started calling me Skinny as a joke. It stuck."

"I'm not sure I like that."

Drea leans over the seat. "I don't like how Shamus got his name either, but you'll learn to roll with it." She gives me a wink and turns to Marlayna, holding a book in her hand. She begins talking with the little girl like she's the most important thing on the planet. Exactly what Marlayna needs. I love that she's getting that from these two.

"Do you all have names like this?"

"Waylon is Triple Threat."

At this I gasp. "What? No, that's not right." Triple Threat means he's dangerous. That just can't be right.

"Yeah, babe. He is. You don't know him now, but you will."

My stomach churns. "I don't think he likes me."

"Why would you say that?"

I shift in my seat. "He doesn't talk to me or anything."

Whitton leans in again. "Roe, he sees how happy you make me. He's workin' through his own shit, but I know for damn sure he doesn't want to be the one to scare you off and away from me."

"No, I wouldn't …"

Whitton interrupts, "Like I said, workin' through stuff. Just know he doesn't hate you. Far from it."

"Okay."

"Ms. Roe?" Marlayna asks from the seat in front of us, pulling Whitton and I out of our conversation.

"Yes, honey."

"Mrs. Easton said I was going to Ms. Marie's house."

Even though I should have expected this, I didn't. Not knowing what's happened to Marie is riding me hard, but I've done my best to keep it in the back of my head. I know Whitton is right. I know she got me in a lot of trouble, and I need to scrape it off. It's just hard for me, but I'm trying.

"Ms. Marie ended up not being able to take you in, honey. It had nothing to do with you at all. Big people sometimes don't make the best decisions, and that's what happened here."

"Sometimes they don't," she says so softly I barely hear. I hate talking to her back, but it is what it is. Eye level would have been better.

"Right," I sigh as Drea reaches over and grabs little Marlayna's hand.

"That's why we got the best present in the entire world, you."

Drea's face beams, and I hope like hell that Marlayna is giving her something back.

"Really?" her little voice says.

"Really. Shamus and I are so happy to have you in our home. You'll have your very own room. I even went to the store and got you a whole set of Barbie bedding to go with your blanket."

"Wow. Does it ..." She trails off and doesn't finish.

"Does it what, sweetheart?" Drea asks.

"Never mind."

I know exactly what she's talking about, and the ache from my past hits hard and tears threaten to fall from my eyes. "Is there a lock?" I ask Drea, already knowing the answer because I helped put the room together, but Marlayna needs to bond with Drea. It's so important that she begins to trust her and Shamus.

A wide smile comes across Drea's face. "Yes. It has a lock."

Damn, I wish I could see the little girl's face. Drea turns to me, a small tear in her eye, and I know this is good. These two with Marlayna will work out perfect.

Marlayna has a family, and I have Whitton. It's everything I could have prayed for. Pastor Corbin would be proud. He saw through our pain. He gave me the motivation to get back to praying. Things may still be new, but we have something and that something is love.

I pause, looking at Shamus checking on his wife and Marlayna in the rearview mirror, and I find myself looking to Whitton.

We have family. It's far more than I could have imagined.

CHAPTER 22

CLOSING IN … THEY'RE GONNA GET MORE THAN THEY
BARGAINED FOR!

Skinny

"Incoming," Shamus calls to me in the back, and I turn to see men on bikes. Not our men and not the Ravage MC. Black Souls. I lift my phone to my ear. "We've got company. Plan B is needed."

"Copy," Thumper says, disconnecting.

"Plan B," I call up to Shamus who nods.

"It's them. Where are we going?" Roe whispers in my ear, I'm pretty sure hoping to not freak out the little girl. Thing Roe needs to know is that little girl has been through hell and if something in her environment changes, she knows it. This is confirmed when Marlayna reaches over to Drea and holds her hand, yet says nothing.

"Thought this would happen. Up the road a ways, we have some back up to get us all out of here."

"Fuck!" Shamus swerves the Tahoe, going off the side of the road and into the gravel. He narrowly misses a large street sign but is able to get over in time. Two men on bikes ride up getting closer and closer, trying to force our hand. Fuck that.

"Do not stop, Shamus," I order, mostly for my own sake because I know Shamus will do what needs to be done.

Roe grabs my hand. I give her a squeeze, release her, and grab my guns.

"Protect her," I tell Roe, knowing she knows this, but giving her the information that this could turn really bad really quickly.

We accelerate, hitting something hard. I feel the rumble beneath us, and I'd be surprised if the cage of the SUV isn't damaged.

"Just a little bump," Shamus says as Drea holds Marlayna against her so she can't see. I watch out the back window as the man and his bike are laying behind us as we go. *Well, that was one way to keep us moving, Shamus*, I think as I assess our situation. It doesn't stop the Black Souls. They come at us again.

"I'm dealin' with this." There are seven or so guys behind us and four to the side of us. "Get down and cover her ears," I order Drea, who complies, quickly pulling the Marlayna out of the seat. Roe climbs over the seat and puts her body over Drea and Marlayna. *We're getting out of this shit.*

I aim at the back window, shattering it. The little girl screams. Drea and Roe try to calm her. I pluck off three guys quickly and they fall to their death, their bikes still moving, then crashing to the ground.

The truck jolts, there's a loud crash that propels me forward hard, almost knocking the gun from my hand.

176

"Fuck!" Shamus yells, pulling out his gun. "Fucker is under the truck." He climbs over the center console and out the passenger side door. Shots are heard under the car. Then shots begin from the Souls.

I grab my two and push out of the side door, using the Tahoe as cover.

"End this shit," Shamus says, and I nod.

Hope Roe knows I love her with all my heart and will do anything and everything to protect her and that little girl. She's my life, my soul forever.

With precise aim, I take out more men at the back, bullets hitting at my feet. Two bikes start to come to our side of the truck. A shot's fired and burning pain sears through my shoulder. I aim right for the guy's head and put him down. His bike drops when he releases the throttle, and he's thrown as gravity takes over. Then move to the next, doing the same.

One of the guy's bikes takes off spinning, hitting the back of the Tahoe and bouncing over our heads and into the grass at the side of the road. We jump out of the way, but it makes us targets. There should be only a few guys left.

Bullets hit the truck, and fear slices through me. This isn't happening. I'm not losing Roe, dammit. Changing the clip quickly, I provide cover while Shamus gets his changed, too.

Shamus and I move to the hood of the truck then get up and start shooting as bullets come flying our way. Just then, bikes come from the right side of us, guns extended and aiming at the four remaining men. My brothers and the Ravage MC. Fuck yeah.

Continuing to shoot, I watch as the assholes fall one by one, crashing to the ground. Once the threat is gone, I open the door to the truck.

"You okay?"

Marlayna is crying, but Roe's head pops up, eyes going wide. "You're shot!"

"You—Roe, Drea, Marlayna. Are you okay?"

Drea rises and Marlayna looks at me, water coming down her face.

"We're fine."

"Little one, all the bad people are gone now. Promise you I'll protect you."

"You will?" The innocence in her eyes reminds me of when I didn't understand what was going on around me as a child.

"Swear it."

CHAPTER 23

PROTECT WHAT'S MINE!

Roe

I push my way out of the truck and focus on Whitton's shoulder. I have no fear. I have no shock. Everything I thought I would feel, I don't. All I think is Whitton is hurt, and I'm glad to see all these men dead because they were trying to take Marlayna and hurt my man. Blood oozes out of his wound showing no sign of stopping. I pull the cardigan from my body and press the fabric to Whitton.

"You're shot!" I repeat.

"No shit, babe," he retorts and if he didn't have a bullet inside of him, I'd slap him. "Roe, it's a clean shot, went all the way through. Just gotta stop the blood, and it'll be fine."

"Fine," I growl. "This is not fine, Whitton Thorne!"

"Roe, are you breathin'?" he asks.

"Yes!" I clip, pressing the cloth harder.

"Drea's breathin', kid's breathin'. Fuck, we're all breathin'. We're family. We knew this shit was a possibility. You knew it was a possibility. It happened, it's done. We deal and move on."

"Is this normal here?"

"I wouldn't say normal, as in an everyday thing, but it happens."

"Man, you alright?" Thumper comes up to Whitton and me.

"Yeah, bullet to the shoulder. Clean through, just need to stop the bleeding," Whitton responds. "Roe's doin' a good job of that." I'm not sure sure about that, but it's a nice thing for him to say.

"Only one man down, that's impressive." A huge man with caramel hair comes up to us. He's dangerous—no other word to describe him. It oozes off of him. "Tahoe's here. Need you, the woman, and kid out of here so we can clean up."

"Right," Whitton answers.

"Who are you?" I ask, seriously suspicious.

"Your ol' lady?" The man asks Whitton, not addressing my question.

"Yeah."

He smiles. "Cruz, president of the Ravage MC. Need ya to get the kid and get out of here so we can take care of this mess."

"Take care of it?"

"Roe," Whitton says, but Cruz continues.

"Yeah, don't need the cops comin' 'round and seein' this shit. We'll get it cleaned up quick if you get the fuck out of here."

I look at Whitton, and he must see the uncertainty in my eyes. "This'll all go away, Roe. It'll just be a memory for you, Drea, and Marlayna."

Something hits me in the gut hard. This is Whitton's life. Shooting people. Killing them. How do I do this?

The ride back to the clubhouse is spent trying to make Marlayna smile. Drea and I break through when we're pretty close to the clubhouse. But it's something, and we'll take it. Drea answered all of Marlayna's questions so appropriately, I thought for sure she should have been a teacher like me. It just made that seal of Marlayna with them so much stronger in my eyes.

Me, I try to keep my thoughts to the little girl beside me. Whitton took the front seat with Shamus driving, and I didn't want to sit by myself.

Unfortunately, it doesn't work, but I did come to a conclusion. Whitton shot at those men because they wanted to hurt us. Wanted to hurt Marlayna. He killed because those men left him no choice. In my eyes, that doesn't make him a bad man. It makes him one that I can depend on to keep all of us safe from the ugly in the world.

It's warped, but I understand it. And I love him all the more for it. His bleeding stopped, and he said the doctor would be at the clubhouse. He called him Bones, and I shivered. I mean … what doctor is named Bones?

His name really doesn't matter, though, as long as he fixes up my man. Yes, my man. I'm in this. I'm in this for the long haul, for now and forever.

CHAPTER 24

ADJUSTED … NEVER BEEN A WORD TO DESCRIBE ME!

THREE WEEKS LATER

"It's perfect," Roe says, staring at the ranch style home that won out in our battle of the houses. I can't tell you how many she drug me through, but we finally found the one. It has four bedrooms, three baths, full basement and three bay garage.

The great thing about me living at the club for so long is I had a lot of cash saved up. Enough pay for this house and be able to get Roe everything she ever wanted.

We stayed with Shamus and Drea for the past three weeks, letting little Marlayna adjust, which she's done well. It was also past time we got out of there and into a place of our own.

Now we have it.

"Yeah, it is."

Horns honk behind us and my brothers are in their trucks, hauling all the shit that Roe picked out. It's time to move in and have a home. With my woman. My Roe.

Everyone's beat and they begin to leave, which is good because I need to christen my fucking house, but I need to take care of something first.

"TT!" I call out and my brother comes in to the kitchen, lifting his chin. We're alone, and I need that for a minute.

"You good about this?"

He gives me a smirk. "Best fuckin' thing that could happen to you, brother. So fuckin' happy you got your home."

"You can get it, too."

"Nah."

I shake my head. "Need to call Roe in here. She thinks you don't like her."

His eyes narrow. "Why the fuck she think that?"

"Because you're so damn personable, TT," I joke.

"Shut the fuck up." He jabs me in the arm, not hard, but I feel it. "Call her."

"Roe!"

Moments later she steps in the room, her eyes darting between me and my brother. "What's going on?"

"TT, you hate Roe?"

Roe's eyes widen. "Whitton! Don't ask him that," she hisses, making me laugh.

TT steps up to Roe, who gets really quiet. "Don't hate you, Roe. So fuckin' happy my brother got back what I cost him. Fuckin' hate I'm the reason he left you in the first place. Gotta live with that. You're the best damn thing that could've happened to him."

"Waylon."

"TT," he corrects her.

184

"TT," she whispers.

"I'm out." He darts from the room so fast you'd swear the man was a magician.

"I didn't even get to tell him anything," Roe says, coming up and wrapping her arms around me.

"Nothin' to say, Roe." I kiss the top of her head. "We have a new bedroom we need to fuck in."

She shivers. The first week after the shooting, she was afraid to touch me. I'm so damn happy she broke out of that.

I pick Roe up bridal style. She screams with excitement as we make our way to the bedroom.

"Good thing we put the bedding on," she says as she falls to the soft grays she picked out.

"Yeah, good thing."

I waste no time and strip her of her clothes, then mine. Her pussy calls to me, and my mouth latches on. She squirms and tries to buck her hips, but my grip is tight, holding her lower half down.

She explodes when I insert my finger the added pressure too much for her. I ride her out while bringing her back up.

Kissing up her body, my lips attack hers and she moans, her hands touching me everywhere. My cock throbs with need.

Instead of sliding home, I flip her over to her hands and knees. She wobbles a bit, getting her balance. Once she finds it, my cock finds its home pressing hard into her. She falls to her elbows, gasping and calling out my name. I love hearing those words off her lips.

Reaching around, I massage her clit quickly as I feel my balls begin to draw up. My head lifts, and my breaths leave me. Our reflection stares back at me in the mirror to the side of the bed. Roe in the throes of passion, me pressing in and out of her. The look of pure ecstasy on my woman's face.

All those years ago, when I took her for the first time, I saw this and never thought in a million years I'd get it back. Now, I have it.

"Roe, look up." Our eyes connect in the mirror. "Best thing that ever happened to me, love you."

She makes a move to speak, but her orgasm takes over and mine follows.

We fall to the bed tangled in each other, breathes uneven, and the smell of sex in the air. Fuckin' heaven.

I reach out and massage her ass. Yeah, love a woman with curves. "Pick a date, Roe."

She moans.

Standing, I go to our bathroom and wet a washcloth with warm water to clean her up. I look in the mirror.

Damn, I smile. This is what happiness is. I feel so full I could burst. Long gone are the days where the weight of the world churns in my stomach. No longer do I wake up with the need to regurgitate my contents because the stress, the evil, and all the wrongs that wreak havoc inside me. The acid is gone and in it's place is love and real, genuine, happiness.

I don't see a scarred man in my reflection. I don't see the evil I was born to be. I see a man with a woman who makes him better, who supports him through it all, and loves him as he is—

marked and all.

Opening the shaving kit, I reach in for the black box I hid a week ago.

Going back to our bed, I trail the wash cloth up the inside of Roe's thighs.

"I could take a nap now," she says, still not turning over. I can't help but laugh.

I roll her over, she stretches her arms over her head as I clean her front and rub her pussy with the cloth. Setting the black box between her legs, she jolts up.

"The guys didn't find my box of toys, did they?" she shrieks, and I laugh as I drop to one knee in front of the bed.

"Loved you then," I begin as she looks between her legs and see the box. "Love your pussy, love your heart, fuckin' love everything that is you, Roelyn Madeline Duprey. Would love to make you my wife. Pick a date, Roe."

Her eyes grow wide. "Whitton Thorne! I can't tell our grandchildren this is how you proposed!"

"Why not?" I laugh.

"Well, first, I can't talk about you loving my pussy, and you keep telling me to pick a date. This is where you're supposed to ask."

I flip the box open and watch as her eyes grow big at the emerald cut solitaire. "Way I see it, I want something, I don't ask—I go for it. I want you to be my wife, so pick a date and we can move onto me lovin' my wife's pussy and showing her everyday how much."

She smiles as I take the ring and slide it on her finger. "Loved you then," I say before kissing the ring and her finger, "fuckin' love you now, and damn sure gonna love you a lifetime."

"I guess I better pick a date," she says, cupping my chin in her hands. "First, show me how much you love me."

I growl and kiss her as I stand and then lay over her. "Say it, Roe, say you'll marry me and then I'll show you how much I love you and your pussy."

"Yes, Whitton Thorne, yes, yes, yes."

SOMETIMES THE GREATEST BATTLE WE FACE IS IN OUR MIND!

Skinny

"Gotta ride out, brother," Triple Threat says from my dining room table.

"Will you be back in time for the wedding?" Roe asks as she sits across from him. This is her thing: once a week, a family meal with my brother. Since TT cleared the air with her, they may not talk but my woman makes sure she includes him in everything she can.

I love the way she accepts him and understands he has his own demons.

"I promise, Roe, nothing will keep me from being there."

The way he looks at me has me on edge. "You aren't one to ride out alone. What's the catch, brother?"

"Made a promise to you a lifetime ago. Won't let her touch you or anything you got again."

My blood runs cold. He's found our mother.

"Nothing's gonna touch me," I try to explain. She's kept her distance over the years. Why the worry now?

"Let's just say I'm gonna make sure of it. The time has come, and she reached out to the wrong people in the wrong way."

Roe's eyes grow wide. "Waylon," she starts, he lifts his hand and she corrects, "TT, please stay with us. No one will bother us."

"I'm gonna make sure of it, sister," he says, trying to soothe my woman.

Standing, he takes his plate to the sink. "Thanks for the food. I'll be back before the wedding." He never says goodbye, it's just not a word he uses. With a squeeze to Roe's shoulder he walks out.

I look at Roe before I stand and follow him out the door. "Way, come on." He turns and his eyes meet mine. The determination in them tells me my brother knows more than he's letting on. "At least let me come with you. Not alone, brother, don't do this alone."

"I took you away from her once, cost you years. Won't do it again." He turns back around, getting to his bike. His final words before the engine roars to life stick with me.

"She took enough from you, I've taken enough from you. Whitt, you've always been the good one. Now, have your life. You're not my keeper anymore."

CATCH UP with all the members of Ruthless Rebels MC in Schooled with Triple Threat and Jessica coming summer 2017!

SNEAK PEAK OF SCHOOLED (RUTHLESS REBELS MC #4)

Waylon "Triple Threat" Thorne – the untouchable.

Man of steel with a capital S

His crystal blue eyes are something dreams are made of down to the way he carries himself, everything is beyond reality.

My first lesson in heartbreak. What happens when we both learn we've been schooled in miscommunications?

Chelsea Camaron and Ryan Michele have teamed up to bring you an explosive new MC romance that will have you panting for more of the Ruthless Rebels. Hold on tight, it's going to be a wild ride full of action and suspense that these two authors are known for. Throw in two people who finally get their second chance, and things are about to get smoking hot.

EXCERPT OF BOUND BY FAMILY BY RYAN MICHELE

Bound By Family (Ravage MC Bound Series #1) ©2017 Ryan Michele

Prologue
Cooper

This life.

My life … is Ravage.

Some say it's my destiny. Others call this my curse.

Lucky for me, I don't give a fuck what anyone thinks. The man I've become is because of a choice—none of that other bullshit. Everyone in life has a choice, a path. What direction you take is up to you.

For me, I had this moment in my life, a moment when I knew who and what I'd become.

It wasn't forced or coerced as the talk has been around this small town. No, the moment that haunts my dreams is what created the man you see today.

Family.

From the beginning to the end, family is what you start with and what you end with. I'm bound to it, honored by it, and respected in it.

Chapter One
Cooper

The echo of the hammer hitting bone crackles through the air in the small, dank room. The man's screams fill the space with pain, anger, and contempt. He doesn't want us here anymore than we want to be in this dump. Unfortunately for us both, he fucked up and it isn't an option. No, it's a necessity.

Fucking Stu.

Ravage Motorcycle Club, my family, we run a tight ship, so to speak. There is a code, rules of sorts that must be followed. Fall out of line, there will be punishment. Stu fell out of line.

Ryker laughs off to the side, pulling me away from my thoughts as I let go of the man's wrist, hammer still clenched in the other hand. The asshole, Stu, falls to his knees on the dirt floor, holding his broken finger.

That's not the only one he's going to get today for his stupidity.

He knows better. Everyone in Sumner, Georgia knows better. Hell, make that anyone who has ever heard of Ravage knows better.

"You've got a hell of a blow with that thing," Ryker calls out. The man is twisted and warped. He does this shit for fun and entertainment. Part of me thinks he gets off on it, but to each their own. Me, I do this shit out of duty and responsibility. Regardless, he's been by my side for years, and I wouldn't have it any other way.

When no response comes from me, Ryker walks up to the man and gives him a savage kick to the gut, making the man curl into a ball to protect himself. Green and Jacks stand off to the side of the small space.

We brought Stu to one of our outbuildings. It's more like a rundown shack, but it has what we need to get the job done.

"I'm thinkin' we need to take off some piggies," Ryker eggs on, and a chuckle escapes me. He does have a way with words, saying exactly what he thinks with not an ounce of filter.

"Give me a shot," Jacks, another one of my brothers and a friend from high school, says as he holds his hand out to me, waiting for the hammer.

Handing it to him, I then take a step back and cross my arms. It's not me being a pussy. It's me wanting to get this shit done so we can get the fuck out of here.

"Money," I bark out to Stu as Ryker gives him another hard kick, this one to his thigh.

Stu owes our club fifty thousand seven hundred dollars and some change for merchandise he purchased. We gave him a week after the initial payment of fifty grand went smooth. Ravage and Stu have a history, and in that time, this is the first instance when Stu hasn't paid up in full. It'll be the last time as well.

"I-I can have it b-by the weekend," Stu stammers out as Jacks swings the hammer, hitting Stu in the ankle. Another crunching sound reverberates throughout the room.

Ryker smirks, coming to stand next to me and giving me a slight bump on the shoulder with his elbow. "Believe this fucker? Weekend?" He shakes his head and spits down at Stu. "Motherfucker, you have twenty-four hours to come up with the cash."

"If we don't have it by then, you're done," I add as Jacks takes another swing.

His cries of fear fill the air.

After an hour of making sure Stu gets the picture by using our fists and hammer, we ride.

***

Fresh air. The freedom of feeling the elements surround me. The delicate balance of navigating a road or eating asphalt.

It's the best part of every day.

The ride.

My bike is a beauty. A Heritage Softtail Harley painted black and red—Ravage MC colors. Working on her has been my pastime for years, tuning and cleaning. I take care of her, and she takes care of me. Wouldn't have it any other way. There's something about taking garbage and turning it into something you love. That's my bike. She began as a pile of shit and turned out to be absolutely perfect.

Life ties us down. Materials hold people back. The open road is about freedom. Ravage is freedom. We live to our code, our standards, and we take care of our own.

My mind clears on the open road awaiting me, nothing but blacktop and paint ahead. Riding allows me the peaceful time to think. Sometimes my rides last hours, while others only last minutes. Normally, whenever my mind figures out what it needs to, that's the time I pull my bike to a stop.

Lately, the Ravage MC has been bringing in some serious money with all the deals that Pops has worked out over the years. Some of them bring more than others, but it's becoming more difficult to filter the money. Especially with the amount of cash. There's only so much we can put through the garage and Studio X, the strip club. Even Stu owes us, and when that cash shows up ... Well, it's got to go somewhere.

It's been working well, but we had to stock pile cash in several of our vaults in the clubhouse basement. Having cash on hand is great in the times we need it, but it will continually increase over time if we keep at this pace. That being said, we need something else to funnel the money.

The thing is, I've been around the club my whole life. I prospected in early. Just turning twenty-two, I've held my place for four years now. I'm ready to step up anywhere needed. More so, I'm ready to give a fresh mindset and view to the way we do business. It's all for family.

My Ravage family.

My top idea is a car wash. It's an all-cash business, unless you let the customers use credit cards, which I would advise against. If we keep it all cash, we could put some of the money through there. I even searched the internet about all the working parts of one of the machines and how much it would take to build and maintain it. Ravage could easily do it, but the downside is all the moving pieces. Sure, we can go and fix the shit, but I want to work smarter, not harder.

There's a way, and I will damn well find it.

My parents taught me many things. The first and foremost is to be my own man. If that means carving a new path for the Ravage MC, I'm up to the task.

***

Pulling up to the clubhouse, we park in the lot, all next to each other, turning off the engines and taking off our helmets.

This building is home.

My memory is damn good, which is both a blessing and a curse. My father doesn't know, but I remember living with my biological mother and seeing stuff as a young child that was flat-out wrong. It's not that he doesn't care to know; we just don't talk about it.

Besides, remembering those times only pisses me off. Seeing men come in and out of the small apartment, going into that woman's bedroom then coming out a while later. She was always doped up on something. Back then, I thought she just wasn't feeling well.

When she started hitting me, that was when I knew what fear was. A woman is supposed to love their kid, at least somewhat. Mine didn't. Not at all.

The moment my father told that woman—my incubator, as we call her now—I was staying with him, that's what I consider my rebirth. It was a new start. Not only that, but I had a new mother, as well. One who loved me, took care of me, and put all my needs above anyone else's, not giving two shits what anyone thought about it.

When I started living, this ugly-as-fuck, cement-blocked building became home. Don't get me wrong, we had a house, as well, but the clubhouse is where it all started for me.

"How'd it go?" Pops, the president of Ravage MC and my grandfather, asks upon us entering the building as I get chin lifts from the guys.

Pops has been the president since I came to Ravage—at least eighteen years. He's done a great job building the Ravage Motorcycle Club into very profitable entities. Not only that, after the bullshit that went down when I was a kid, Pops keeps a tight leash on any and all our friends and enemies. One doesn't do what we do and not have a huge basket of both, but Pops has kept it all in line.

"Ryker got a little too happy, so the guy won't be having kids, probably ever, but the message was sent. If he doesn't have it by the weekend, then we'll take care of it."

Pops chuckles.

"Hey, the fucker was tryin' to stand up. If he would've stayed down, his nuts wouldn't have cracked."

Laughter is heard throughout the clubhouse.

Pops slaps his hand on my shoulder, giving it a squeeze. The look he gives me is different, but he says nothing as he walks to one of the tables and has a seat.

I've noticed things about him these last few months. The looks that come across his face when he thinks no one is looking, as if he's tired and the weight of the world rests on his shoulders. There's no doubt in my mind that it's true.

Running an entire MC is a shit-ton of work. Even doing it for years and having it down pat, there comes a time when it could be too much. I kept my mouth shut about it, though, not wanting to overstep my boundaries. When Pops is ready to tell us what's going on, he will.

Heading toward the bar, I grasp the cold beer sitting on it then join the guys at the table. Blood means nothing to any of us. We are a family of our own choosing. Each one of us couldn't be more different if we tried. It's as if we were put together in this clubhouse for a reason.

Take Becs. He's the vice president and has recently told us that he'd like to step down and let one of the younger guys take his role. That decision is huge and one of the highest topics at our next church. Becs is quiet. Silent but deadly. He's never up in your face, but one wrong move, and he will tear you down.

Then there's Rhys. He's silent, but his face, body—hell, even the air around him—screams "breath my air, and I'll end you."

My dad, Cruz, he's middle road between the two. He has no problem getting in someone's face, yet he'll only do it when necessary. His face isn't scary like Rhys', but he has his own badass vibe he puts off.

Me, I'm more of a thinker, a planner if you will. I like to look at all the possibilities and facts before coming up with a strategy.

Somehow, all our crazy asses fit together, and we are bound by family.

Read   more   in   Bound   by   Family
www.authorrymichele.net

202

EXCERPT OF IN THE RED (DEVIL'S DUE MC #1) BY CHELSEA CAMARON

In The Red (Devil's Due MC Book 1)
©2016 Chelsea Camaron

The event that shook one small town to its core was never solved. The domino effect of one person's crime going unpunished is beyond measure.

He's no saint.

Dover 'Collector' Ragnes rides with only five brothers at his back. Nomads with no place to call home, they never stay in one place too long. Together, they are the Devil's Due MC, and their only purpose is to serve justice their way for unsolved crimes everywhere they go.

She's not afraid to call herself a sinner.

Emerson Flint still remembers the loss of her elementary school best friend. She is all grown up, but the memories still haunt her of the missing girl. Surrounding herself with men at the tattoo shop, she never questions her safety. Her life is her art. Her canvas is the skin of others.

However, danger is at her door.

Will Dover overcome the history he shares with Emerson in time? Will Emerson lead him to the retribution he has always sought?

Love, hate, anger, and passion collide as the time comes, and the devil demands his due.

Prologue

I hang my head and sit in silence. The television blares as strangers move about our house. Some of them are trying to put together a search party, and others are here with food and attempts to comfort. I want them all to go away. I want to scream or break something. I want them all to stop looking at me like I should be beaten within an inch of my life then allowed to heal, only to get beaten again. Do I deserve that?

Hell yes, I do, and more.

There is no reprieve from the hell we are in. I would sell my soul to the Devil himself if I could turn back time. Only, I can't.

The reporter's voice breaks through all of the clamor.

"In local news tonight, a nine-year-old girl is missing, and authorities are asking for your help. Raleigh Ragnes was last seen by her seventeen-year-old brother. According to her parents, her brother was watching her afterschool when the child wandered outside and down the street on her pink and white bicycle with streamers on the handlebars.

"She was last known to have her brown hair braided with a yellow ribbon tied at the bottom. She was in a yellow shirt and a black denim dress that went to her knees. She wore white Keds with two different color laces; one is pink, and one is purple.

"There is a reward offered for any information leading to the successful return of Raleigh to her

home. Any information is appreciated and can be given by calling the local sheriff's department."

The television seems to screech on and on with other reports as if our world hasn't just crumbled. My mom's sobs only grow louder.

God, I'm an ass. Raleigh was whining all afternoon about going to Emerson's house. Those two are practically inseparable. She had made the trip numerous times to the Flint's home at the end of the cul-de-sac, so I didn't think twice about her leaving.

Gretchen was here, locked in my room with me. My hand was just making it down her pants when I yelled at Raleigh through the door to just go, not wanting the distraction. My mind was only occupied with getting into Gretchen's pants.

Only, while I was making my way to home base, my little sister never made it to her friend's house. None of us knew until dinner time arrived and my sister never came home. The phone call to Emerson's sent us all into a tailspin.

While other families watch the eleven o'clock news to simply be informed, for my family, my little sister is the news.

~Three weeks later ~

The television screeches once again. I thought the world had crumbled before, but now it's crushed and beyond repair. The reporter's tone is not any different than if they were giving the local weather as the words they speak crash through my ears.

"In local news tonight, the body of nine-year-old Raleigh Ragnes was found in a culvert pipe under Old Mill Road. Police are asking for anyone with any

information to please come forward. The case is being treated as an open homicide."

In the matter of a month, my sister went from an innocent little girl to a case number, and in time, she will be nothing more than a file in a box. Everyone else may have called it cold and left it unsolved, but that's not who I am.

The domino effect of one person's crime going unpunished is beyond measure.

Chapter One
~Dover~

Giving up is not an option for me ... It never has been.

"There's a time and a place to die, brother," I say, scooping Trapper's drunk ass up off the dirty floor of the bar with both my hands under his armpits. "This ain't it."

It's a hole in the wall joint, the kind we find in small towns everywhere. It's a step above a shack on the outside, and the inside isn't much better: one open room, linoleum floor from the eighties. The bar runs the length of the space with a pair of saloon-style swinging doors closing off the stock room. We have gotten shit-faced in nicer, and we have spent more than our fair share of time in worse.

At the end of a long ride, a cold beer is a cold beer. Really, it doesn't matter to us where it's served as long as it has been on ice and is in a bottle.

"I'm nowhere near dying," he slurs, winking at the girl he has had on his lap for the last hour. She's another no name come guzzler in a slew of many we find throughout every city, town, and stop we make. "In fact, I'm not far from showing sweet thing here a little piece of heaven."

"Trapper." Judge, the calmest of us all, gets in his face. "She rode herself to oblivion until you fell off the stool. She's done got hers, man. Time to get you outta here so you can have some quality time huggin' Johnny tonight."

We all laugh as Trapper tries to shake me off. "Fuck all y'all. That pussy is mine tonight."

"Shithead, sober up. She's off to the bathroom to snort another line, and she won't be coming back for another ride on your thigh. Time to go, brother," Rowdy says sternly.

Trapper turns to the redheaded, six-foot, six-inch man of muscle and gives him a shit-eating grin. "Aw, Rowdy, are you gonna be my sober sister tonight?"

I wrap my arm around Trapper, pulling him into a tight hold. "Shut your mouth now!"

He holds up his hands in surrender, and we make our way out of the bar.

Another night, another dive. Tomorrow is a new day and a new ride.

Currently, we are in Leed, Alabama for a stop off. The green of the trees, the rough patches of the road—it all does nothing to bring any of us out of the haunting darkness we each carry.

We're nomads—no place to call home, and that's how we like it. The six of us have been a club of our own creation for almost two years now. We all have a story to tell. We all have a reason we do what we do. None of us are noble or honorable. We strike in the most unlikely of places and times, all based on our own brand of rules and systems.

Fuck the government. Fuck their laws. And damn sure fuck the judicial system.

Once your name is tainted, no matter how good you are, you will never be clean in the eyes of society. I'm walking, talking, can't sleep at night proof of it. Well, good fucking deal. I have learned society's version of clean is everything I don't ever want to be.

The scum that blends into our communities and with our children, the cons that can run a game, they think they are untouchable. The number of crimes outnumber the crime fighters. The lines between law abiding and law breaking blur every day inside every precinct. I know, because I carried the badge and thought I could be a change in the world. Then I found out everything is just as corrupt for the people upholding the law as those breaking it.

Day in and day out, watching cops run free who deserve to be behind bars more than the criminals they put away takes its toll. Everyone has a line in the sand, and once they cross it, they don't turn back. I found mine, and I found the brotherhood in the Devil's Due MC. Six guys who have all seen our own fair share of corruption in the justice system. Six guys who don't give a fuck about the consequences.

Well, that's where me and my boys ride in. No one's above the devil getting his due. We are happy to serve up our own kind of punishments that most certainly fit the crimes committed, and we don't bother with the current legal system's view of justice served.

We're wayward souls, damaged men, who have nothing more than vengeance on our minds.

"Fucking bitch, she got my pants wet," Trapper says, just realizing she really did get off on his thigh and left him behind. "You see this shit?" He points at his leg.

Trapper mad is good. He will become focused rather than let the alcohol keep him in a haze. He could use some time to dry up. He's sharp. His attention to detail saves our asses in city after city. However, things get too close to home when we ride to the deep south like this, and he can't shake the ghosts in the closets of his mind. At five-foot-ten and a rock solid one eighty-five, he's a force of controlled power. He uses his brain more than his brawn, but he won't back down in a brawl, either.

We help him get outside the dive bar we spent the last two hours inside, tossing beer back and playing pool. Outside, the fresh winter air hits him, and he shakes his head.

"It's not that cold," X says, slapping Trapper in the face. "Sober up, sucka."

Trapper smiles as he starts to ready his mind. As drunk as he is, he knows he has to have his head on straight to ride.

"Flank him on either side, but stay behind in case he lays her down. We only have four miles back to the hotel," I order, swinging my leg over my Harley

Softail Slim and cranking it. The rumble soothes all that stays wound tight inside me. The vibration reminds me of the power under me.

Blowing out a breath, I tap the gas tank. "Ride for Raleigh," I whisper and point to the night sky. *Never forget*, I remind myself before I move to ride. My hands on the bars, twisting the throttle, I let the bike move me and lift my feet to rest on the pegs. As each of my brother's mount, I pull out, knowing they will hit the throttle and catch me, so I relax as the road passes under me.

We ride as six with no ties to anyone or anything from one city to the next. We have a bond. We are the only family for each other, and we keep it that way. No attachments, no commitments, and that means no casualties.

We are here by choice. Any man can leave the club and our life behind at any time. I trust these men with my life and with my death. When my time is called, they will move on with the missions as they come.

We don't often let one another drink and drive, but coming south, Trapper needed to cut loose for a bit. He may be drunk, yet once the wind hits his face, he will be solid. He always is.

At the no-tell motel we are crashing at, X takes Trapper with him to one of the three shit-ass rooms we booked while Judge and Rowdy go to the other. The place has seen better days, probably thirty years ago. It's a place to shit, shower, and maybe, if I can keep the nightmares away, sleep. I have never needed anything fancy, and tonight is no different.

I give them a half salute as they close their doors and lock down for the night.

Deacon heads on into our room. Always a man of few words and interaction, he doesn't look back or give me any indication that he cares if I follow or stay behind.

I give myself the same moment I take every night and stand out under the stars to smoke.

I look up. Immediately, I can hear her tiny voice in my mind, making up constellations all her own. Raleigh was once a rambunctious little girl. She was afraid of nothing. She loved the night sky and wishing upon all the stars.

Another city, another life, I wish it was another time, but one thing I know is that there is no turning back time. If I could, I would. Not just for me, but for all five of us.

I light my cigarette and take a deep drag. Inhaling, I hold it in my lungs before I blow out. The burn, the taste, and the touch of it to my lips don't ease the thoughts in my mind. Another night is upon us, and it's yet another night Raleigh will never come home.

The receptionist steps out beside me. She isn't the one who was here when we checked in earlier. When she smiles up at me, I can tell she has been waiting on us. Guess the trailer trash from day shift chatted up her replacement. Well, at least this one has nice teeth. Day shift definitely doesn't have dental on her benefit plan here.

"Go back inside," I bark, not really in the mood for company.

"I'm entitled to a break," she challenges with a southern drawl.

"If you want a night with a biker, I'm not the one," I try to warn her off.

"Harley, leather, cigarettes, and sexy—yeah, I think you're the one ... for tonight, that is." She comes over and reaches out for the edges of my cut.

I grab her wrists. "You don't touch my cut."

She bites her bottom lip with a sly smile. "Oh, rules. I can play by the rules, big daddy."

I drop her hands and walk in a circle around her before standing in front of her then backing her to the wall. I take another drag of my cigarette and blow the smoke into her face. "I'm not your fucking daddy." I take another long drag. Smoke blows out with each word as I let her know. "If you wanna fuck, we'll fuck. Make no mistake, though, I'm not in the mood to chat, cuddle, or kiss. I'm a man; I'll fuck, and that's it."

She leans her head back, testing me.

"Hands against the wall," I order, and she slaps her palms against the brick behind her loudly.

Her chest rises and falls dramatically as her breathing increases. She keeps licking and biting her lips.

"You want a ride on the wild side?"

She nods, pushing her tits out at me.

"You wet for me?" I ask, and she giggles while nodding. "If you want me to get hard and stay hard, you don't fucking make a sound. That giggling shit is annoying as fuck."

Immediately, she snaps her mouth shut.

I yank her shirt up and pull her bra over her titties without unhooking it. Her nipples point out in the cold night air.

"You cold or is that for me?" I ask, flicking her nipple harshly.

"You," she whispers breathlessly.

I yank the waistband of her stretchy pants down, pulling her panties with them. Her curls glisten with her arousal under the street light.

With her pants at her ankles, I turn her around to face the wall.

"Bend over, grab your ankles. You don't speak, don't touch me, and you don't move. If you want a wild ride with a biker, I'm gonna give you one you'll never forget."

While she positions herself, I grab a condom from my wallet and unbutton my four button jeans enough to release my cock. While stroking myself a few times to get fully erect, part of me considers just walking away. However, I'm a man, and pussy is pussy. No matter what my mood, it's a place to sink into for a time.

Covering myself carefully, I spread her ass cheeks and slide myself inside her slick cunt.

The little whore is more than ready.

I close my eyes and picture a dark-haired beauty with ink covering her arms and a tight cunt made just for me. I can almost hear the gravelly voice of my dream woman as she moans my name, pushing back to take me deeper, thrust after thrust.

I roll my hips as the receptionist struggles to keep herself in position.

214

Raising my hand, I come down on the exposed globe of her ass cheek. "Dirty fucking girl." I spank her again. "I'm not your fucking daddy, but I'll give you what he obviously didn't." I spank her again and thrust. "Head down between your legs. Watch me fuck your pussy."

She does as instructed and watches as I continue slamming into her. Stilling, I reach down and twist her nipples as she pushes back on me.

Her moans get louder as I move, gripping her hips and pistoning in and out of her.

I slap her ass again. "I said quiet."

I push deep, my hips hitting her ass, and she shakes as her orgasm overtakes her.

"Fuck me!" she wails.

I slam in and out, in and out, faster and faster, until I explode inside the condom.

She isn't holding her ankles by the time I'm done. She's still head down, bent over with her back against the wall as her hands hang limply like the rest of her body, trembling in aftershocks.

Pulling out, I toss the condom on the ground and walk away, buttoning my pants back up.

"Collector," I hear X yell my road name from his doorway. "You ruined that one." He is smoking a cigarette. It's obvious he watched the show.

The noise has Judge coming to his door and giving me a nod of approval.

I look over my shoulder to see the bitch still hasn't moved. Her pussy is out in the air, ass up, head down, and she's still moaning. Desperate, needy, it's not my thing.

"I need a shower," I say, giving X a two finger salute before going into my own room. Deacon is already in bed and doesn't move as I go straight back to the shit-ass bathroom to clean up.

I wasn't lying. I smell like a bar, and now I smell the skank stench of easy pussy. I have needs, but I can't help wondering what it would be like to have to work for my release just once. It's not in my cards, though. Just like this town, this ride, and that broad, it's on to the next for me and my bothers of the Devil's Due MC.

ABOUT CHELSEA CAMARON

USA Today bestselling author Chelsea Camaron is a small town Carolina girl with a big imagination. She's a wife and mom, chasing her dreams. She writes contemporary romance, erotic suspense, and psychological thrillers. She loves to write about blue-collar men who have real problems with a fictional twist. From mechanics to bikers to oil riggers to smokejumpers, bar owners, and beyond she loves a strong hero who works hard and plays harder.

www.authorchelseacamaron.com

chelseacamaron@gmail.com

OTHER BOOKS BY CHELSEA CAMARON

Love and Repair Series: Available in KU
Crash and Burn
Restore My Heart
Salvaged
Full Throttle
Beyond Repair
Stalled
Box Set Available

Hellions Ride Series:
One Ride
Forever Ride
Merciless Ride
Eternal Ride
Innocent Ride
Simple Ride
Heated Ride
Ride with Me (Hellions MC and Ravage MC Duel
with Ryan Michele)
Originals Ride
Final Ride

Roughneck Series: Available in KU
Maverick
Heath
Lance

Box Set Available

Stand Alone Thriller –
Stay

Stand Alone Short Romance –
Serving My Soldier
Mother Trucker

Devil's Due MC Series:
Crossover
In The Red
Below The Line
Close The Tab (Coming Soon)

The following series are co-written
The Fire Inside Series:
(co-written by Theresa Marguerite Hewitt)
Kale

Regulators MC Series:
(co-written by Jessie Lane)
Ice
Hammer
Coal

Summer of Sin Series
Original Sin (co-written with Ripp Baker, Daryl
Banner, Angelica Chase, MJ Fields, MX King)

Caldwell Brothers Series
(co-written by USA Today Bestselling Author MJ
Fields)
Hendrix
Morrison
Jagger

Stand Alone Romance – co-written with MJ Fields
Visibly Broken
Use Me

Ruthless Rebels MC Series –
co-written with Ryan Michele
Shamed
Scorned
Scarred
Schooled (coming soon)

ABOUT RYAN MICHELE

Ryan Michele found her passion in bringing fictional characters to life. She loves being in an imaginative world where anything is possible, and she has a knack for special twists readers don't see coming.

She writes MC, Contemporary, Erotic, Paranormal, New Adult, Inspirational, and other romance-based genres. Whether it's bikers, wolf-shifters, mafia, etc., Ryan spends her time making sure her heroes are strong and her heroines match them at every turn.

When she isn't writing, Ryan is a mom and wife living in rural Illinois and reading by her pond in the warm sun.

www.authorryanmichele.net

ryanmicheleauthor@gmail.com

OTHER BOOKS BY RYAN MICHELE

Ravage MC Series
Ravage Me
Seduce Me
Consume Me
Inflame Me
Captivate Me
Ravage MC Novella Collection
Ride with Me (co-written with Chelsea Camaron)

Ravage MC Bound Series
Bound by Family
Bound by Desire (June 20, 2017)

Vipers Creed MC Series
Challenged
Conquering
Conflicted (Coming soon)

Ruthless Rebels MC Series (co-written with Chelsea Camaron) Available in KU
Shamed
Scorned
Scarred
Schooled (Coming Soon)

Loyalties Series
Blood & Loyalties: A Mafia Romance

Raber Wolf Pack Series (Available in KU)
Raber Wolf Pack Book 1
Raber Wolf Pack Book 2
Raber Wolf Pack Book 3

Stand Alone Romances Available in KU
Full Length Novels
Needing to Fall
Safe
Wanting You

Short Stories Available in KU
Hate Sex
Branded

Billionaire Romance Series
Stood Up
Set Up (Coming Soon)
Picked Up (Coming Soon)
Hung Up (Coming Soon)
www.authorryanmichele.net

DON'T MISS A RELEASE

Come join Chelsea Camaron and Ryan Michele in our groups on Facebook
Chelsea Camaron
Ryan Michele

Want to be up to date on all New Releases? Sign up for our Newsletter
Chelsea Camaron
Ryan Michele

Made in the USA
Monee, IL
27 November 2023